"Oh, c'mon," Alexis protested, trying to twist out of her sister's grip. "This is high school, Fabi. I want to have fun. Do crazy things."

"You *will* do crazy things," Fabi said. "I promise. But trust me on this: You don't want to do them with Dex."

Alexis's eyes lit up. "That's his name? Dex. Dex what?"

"Dex Nada, because that boy is *nada* to you. Listen," Fabi said with a sigh. "Look, you've just got to trust me on this one. I'll explain at lunch, okay?" Then she hurried away to her own classroom on the second floor.

border town

Crossing the Line

Quince Clash

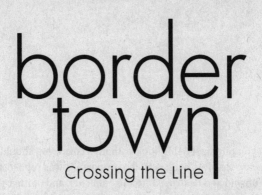

border town

Crossing the Line

MALÍN ALEGRÍA

Point

No part of this publication may be reproduced, stored in a retrieval system, or transmitted in any form or by any means, electronic, mechanical, photocopying, recording, or otherwise, without written permission of the publisher. For information regarding permission, write to Scholastic Inc., Attention: Permissions Department, 557 Broadway, New York, NY 10012.

ISBN 978-0-545-40240-8 (Trade) / ISBN 978-0-545-46045-3 (BF)

Copyright © 2012 by Malín Alegría
All rights reserved. Published by Point, an imprint of Scholastic Inc.
SCHOLASTIC, POINT, and associated logos are trademarks and/or registered trademarks of Scholastic Inc.

12 11 10 9 8 7 6 5 4 3 2 1   12 13 14 15 16 17/0

Printed in the U.S.A.   23
First Printing, May 2012

Pueblo chico,
infierno grande.

Small town,
big hell.

chapter 1

"It's really no big deal," Fabiola Garza told herself. "Just grab it and go."

She snatched the small package and headed straight for the front of the drugstore. She walked quickly, her hot-pink *chanclas* slapping loudly against the linoleum floor. Despite the noise, Fabi tried to stroll through the store nonchalantly, careful not to make eye contact with any of the customers. Her heart was beating so hard it felt like it was going to burst out of her chest.

She stopped at the end of the aisle. There were three clerks ringing up customers. Down at the far end stood a new girl. Fabi rushed over to her line.

"In and out," she repeated softly to herself like a mantra.

The new girl wasn't having a good day. Her eyes swept from Fabiola to the end of the line with a pained grin, then suddenly back to her register with alarm. She'd been written up twice that week, and had already made several careless mistakes today. The register beeped ERROR at her. The cashier huffed loudly and started to reenter the item code. *Beep*. "Darn it, not again!" the girl exclaimed. The customers in line in front of Fabi started to grumble and complain.

"Fabiola!" a familiar voice called out.

For a split second Fabi tried to ignore whoever was calling her. She did not want to bump into anyone she knew — especially now. But the person was persistent.

"Fabiola Garza, is that you?"

The woman behind her nudged Fabi and said in Spanish, "Excuse me, I think that man is talking to you," as she pointed to one of the other cash registers.

Fabi turned and saw a thin man with no hair and a big, bushy mustache. Mr. Longoria, her old Sunday school teacher! He waved eagerly at her with a bright, toothy smile and a red sales rep vest. "I'm open, and you're next in line." He motioned for her to come. "Bring your stuff over here."

Fabi's cheeks burned hot. "Oh, it's okay. I can wait."

Mr. Longoria made a face and waved off her explanation. "Don't be silly," he said.

Fabi looked for the nearest exit. Maybe she could still make a run for it, she thought — but her feet would not cooperate. She stood motionless, like a deer in headlights.

"Go ahead," the woman behind her said. "You only have one thing."

Fabi's sandals edged forward. Her mind went blank. How was she going to explain this? She had to make up something quick.

"My, have you grown!" Mr. Longoria said with amazement as she approached his cash register. "How's your mother? And your grandmother Trini? I haven't seen her in years."

Maybe he won't notice, she half hoped. *Maybe he won't care?* Fabi watched as Mr. Longoria's hairy hand slowly reached for her package. She stared at the big horseshoe ring on his middle finger. But she couldn't let go of the small pink box.

"Is everything all right?" he asked, concern growing on his face.

"No, I just have a little headache. Everything is fine," Fabi said, shaking her fears loose. She threw the box down quickly and sought a conversation in hopes of distracting him. Leaning over the counter and holding on to his gaze, she blurted, "My grandma Trini just got back from Las Vegas — all expenses paid, you know."

Mr. Longoria shook his head, smiling to himself. He grabbed her item without looking and passed it over the scanner. "Your grandma is the luckiest woman I —" He paused and frowned at the box. It hadn't scanned. "That's strange," he said. He tried it again.

"You know what?" Fabi paused, and said a bit too loudly, "I changed my mind. I don't want it anymore."

"Oh, it's no problem," Mr. Longoria told her, picking up the phone. Fabi's heart started to race. "Petra," he called out casually into the receiver. His voice echoed loudly throughout the store on the PA system. "I've got Fabiola Garza up here. You know, Trinidad Garza's grand-daughter. I need a price check on the *Fresh Mountain Scented Gentle Glide Super Plus Tampons* for her."

Fabi shot out through the front door and into the parking lot. The stifling heat smacked her face, arms, and legs like fiery brands. She rushed, heart pounding, toward the black Ford truck that was idling by the entrance. Her cousin Santiago was sitting at the wheel, busily texting, as she climbed in.

"Did you get what you needed?" Santiago asked, smiling. A hint of mischief lurked in his honey-colored eyes. As usual. All the girls at school mooned over Santiago like he was Christmas Day. His dark black curls attracted women — young and old — like bees to sweet nectar. To Fabi he was just Santiago, her favorite cousin. And she knew him well enough to guess that he must have been texting some new girl.

"Just drive," she said, urgently waving him forward. Fabi wanted to get as far away from this place as possible.

Suddenly, Mr. Longoria burst through the storefront doors. He called out to her, "Fabiola! Wait! Stop!" as he waved the box of tampons in the air for the whole world to see.

"Go!" Fabi shrieked again, hitting the dashboard with her palms. "Go right now!"

Santiago didn't ask any questions. He pressed down on the accelerator and quickly exited the parking lot, leaving a bewildered-looking Mr. Longoria behind in a cloud of dust and car fumes.

"Ooooh!" Santiago cried, laughing. "Did you just steal something? No, you held the place up. Damn, Fabi, you crazy. You are SO going to get it when your mom finds out."

Fabi dug her fingernails into her fists. "It's nothing like that," she said between clenched teeth.

"Then what was it?"

"Nothing."

"Didn't look like nothing to me."

Fabiola folded her arms in front of her chest and looked out onto the arid, flat landscape. She watched as they sped past the leafy, low-growing mesquite trees and prickly pear cactus plants scattered along the state highway. When she was younger, her grandpa Frank would take her out to see the migratory birds returning from the south. He knew every plant and animal in the Valley. Ten miles to the south was Mexico, and ten miles to the north was stark, rocky wilderness dotted with thirsty tasajillo brush, jackrabbits, and squawking mockingbirds.

But Fabi couldn't enjoy the calming landscape. She was so irritated she wanted to scream. This was exactly why she hated living in the Valley. You couldn't do *anything* without running into someone you knew! Naively she'd thought she could be anonymous if she made Santiago drive her two towns over. But there was no such thing as "anonymous" along the Rio Grande.

Santiago flipped through the channels on the radio until he found a tune he knew would cheer her up.

"Ooooooh, baby," he sang out, really loud and really off-key. "So let's go on and on and on."

Fabi tried to stay mad. But Santiago was so horribly tone-deaf that she couldn't hold back her smile. "You are such a dork," she mumbled.

He glanced at her sideways. "But I'm a cute dork, huh?" he said, nudging her playfully. "C'mon, sing with me." Fabi tried to resist, but Santiago always found a way to make her forget her troubles. He raised the volume and she joined him. They both sang out, bobbing back and forth with the chorus.

Santiago parked in front of a green brick storefront in the middle of old downtown. A chipped, weather-beaten sign that said "Garza's" hung over the doorway. Cartoon depictions of their family restaurant's famous specialties were painted on the side of the wall: fajitas, enchiladas, cabrito, tacos, flautas, crispy chalupas. And of course there was also the painting of Grandma Alpha, holding a plate of her famous mouthwatering chili.

"You comin' in?" Fabi asked, opening the truck's passenger-side door.

Santiago made a face, as if he was thinking really hard about it. Then his thoughts shifted instantly as his phone beeped. He glanced quickly at it and smiled. "I'd love to, but I got this thing I have to do first."

"What's this one's name?" Fabi said, feigning boredom. Her cousin had so many girlfriends she couldn't keep track of them. She shut the door but kept looking at him through the open window.

Santiago gave her his famous smile. "Maria Elena," he said, overenunciating her name in a deep Spanish accent.

"She sounds dangerous," Fabi joked.

"I hope so," he yelled as he sped off.

Fabiola shook her head; her cousin was incorrigible. Then she just stood in front of the restaurant for a second, enjoying the relative calm of downtown Dos Rios in the noon sun. Abandoned mannequins stared down at her from the old JC Ramirez Fashion Boutique. Most of the stores were deserted. Only three hung on — a food stamp office, a storefront with the sign "Aquí Es" that sold diet shakes, and the restaurant. Locals no longer came downtown to shop, preferring the big chains in McAllen for their daily needs.

Fabi took a deep breath before pushing open the glass door of her family's restaurant. *Norteño* music sang out from the old jukebox. More paintings — murals by her uncle Neto — covered the walls with images of the Aztec empire, Pancho Villa riding a white stallion, and Cesar Chavez leading farmworkers in a protest march. On the wall behind the cash register there were old photographs of long-dead ancestors, mixed with recent pictures of other family members taken with celebrities, like Hulk Hogan, Selena, and Freddy Fender. Fabi breathed in the thick aroma of grilled steak, caramelized onions, and freshly cooked beans. Pots and pans clanged noisily in the kitchen over the boisterous chatter of regular customers seated at all the red tables and counter spaces. Fabi's mom,

Magdalena (whom everyone called Magda), was talking to a couple of Winter Texans at the register counter when she noticed Fabi.

"Mija!" she called out. "Where've you been? Your dad has been looking for you. Lydia and Lorena called in sick. Pig flu, they say! *Mentirosas,"* she said, giving the elderly man in a Hawaiian shirt his change with a broad smile. As the customers walked away, Magda leaned over the glass counter and whispered, "I know those two girls were dancing on tables at Long Horns last night. Everybody saw them acting all *chifladas."* The phone rang and her mom hurriedly shooed Fabi away, adding, *"Ándale,* get your apron."

Fabi walked to the opposite side of the counter with a small smile. She couldn't wait to hear about her coworkers' latest adventure. Her grandpa Frank sat on a stool drinking a cup of lukewarm coffee — just the way he liked it. She leaned over and gave him a big kiss on his saggy cheek.

"No sugar for your *abuelita*?" grumbled Abuelita Alpha Omega from her table in the corner. Alpha wore her white hair tied back in a bun so tight it made her eyelids slant. In her arms, she rocked Fabi's two-year-old baby brother. His name was Rafael, although everyone called him Baby Oops.

"Ay, Abuelita," Fabiola teased, "I was just about to come over." As she moved toward her demanding-but-beloved grandmother, she grabbed an apron from behind the counter.

"Fabi!" her father's stern voice rang out from the kitchen. "Is that you?"

"You better go see what he wants," her *abuelita* warned. "He's been in a foul mood ever since he got back from the doctor."

Fabiola pecked her grandmother on the cheek. Then, hands twisting quickly above her head, she tied her long black hair into a neat bun. "Coming, Dad!"

"Oh, so now you only kiss your mama's side of the family?" another familiar voice called out from the opposite end of the room. It was her dad's mom, Trinidad Garza. This *abuela* sat majestically next to a wall-high shrine to Fabi's late grandfather, Little Rafa "Los Dedos del Valle" Treviño Garza.

Fabi rushed over to her other grandmother, who smelled of hair spray and Jean Naté perfume. It was especially important not to show any favoritism in their family since the Great Truce of 2008, when both grandmothers finally agreed to get along — as long as each stayed on her half of the restaurant.

"Sorry, Grandma," said Fabi, rushing over to give her other grandmother a quick kiss, while being *extra* careful not to ruin any makeup. "How's business?" Fabi asked her.

Grandma Trini was wearing a "Little Rafa" T-shirt. The shirt was a tad too small, emphasizing her large and rather perky chest. The table in front of her was filled with miniature replicas of the icon himself: Little Rafa, with his long cascading mullet, cheerfully playing his accordion.

There were also T-shirts, buttons, key chains, and Grandma Trini's assortment of crocheted steering wheel covers, hats, and doilies.

"We had some tourists from Germany come in," Grandma Trini told Fabi excitedly. "Came all the way out here just to pay their respects. He's real big in Strasburg, they said. They bought two shirts and a button and took pictures with me." She pinned a button with Little Rafa's face onto Fabi's apron. "Can't sell what you don't show. Like it? I've got more. Maybe you can sell them at your school? Think your friends might like them?"

"Yeah, sure." Fabi looked for an escape.

"Can I get some help back here?" her dad yelled from the kitchen, just in time.

Fabiola smiled at her grandmother. "I gotta go. My dad wants me."

"Okay, honey. Don't you worry, I save some pins for you, okay?"

"Fabi, take the orders out," her mother called.

"Fabiola!" her dad echoed.

"I'm coming!" Fabi yelled back. She hurried over to the kitchen and grabbed a hot plate of chicken fajitas and an order of enchiladas from the counter. Her dad, Leonardo, was expertly moving around, stirring a huge pot of whole pinto beans, slicing red bell peppers, and flipping fresh corn tortillas on the hot *comal*.

Leonardo had started life as a migrant kid picking fruits and vegetables from South Texas to Minnesota. Owning a restaurant had been just a dream. He and Magda had put twenty years of sweat, tears, and sometimes blood into the business. All of Fabi's childhood memories revolved around this place. It was all she knew.

"Mija," her mother cried again over the diners' chatter. "Mr. Longoria just called."

Fabi stopped in her tracks, hot full plates suspended over her head.

"You okay, *mija*?" her mother asked, cleaning down the glass counter that held Mexican candies, cigarettes, and other trinkets.

"I think I'm going to be sick."

Her mother continued on, ignoring the look of utter horror on Fabi's face. "He said something about a box of tampons. Do you know what he's talking about?"

"Tapón?" asked Grandpa Frank, who was hard of hearing. "Get some prune juice, *mija*, if you're *tapada*."

"No, I said 'tampon,' not '*tapón*'!" her mom corrected him, loud enough for the whole restaurant to stop all conversation and stare at Fabi in a hushed silence.

Fabi felt all the blood drain from her face. "Oh, no," she groaned to herself.

"Tampons?" cried Abuelita Alpha. "Nooooo. Good girls don't use that stuff. It makes you lose your virginity. That's for *pirujas*!"

The customers, many of whom Fabi had grown up with, broke their abrupt silence with sudden roars of laughter.

"Not true," called Grandma Trini from the opposite side of the room. She jumped up and

[17]

took the tray of hot plates from Fabi, setting it down on the nearest table. Fabiola sighed with relief, as she'd completely forgotten about the orders she'd been holding.

The customers at the table next to her protested that they hadn't ordered those plates, but Grandma Trini told them this was better, to stop complaining and eat. Then she turned back to Fabi and petted her hand, looking down pointedly, her sparkly false eyelashes fluttering. "*Mija*, we need to talk about what goes on down there, so that you don't hurt yourself."

Fabi jumped back. *This cannot be happening*, she thought.

"Magda," yelled Grandma Trini over Fabi's head, "have you had THE TALK . . . you know . . . boys . . . and the stuff that happens *down there*? We should have THE TALK. I remember when I was her age . . ."

Fabi felt her ears burning. She just wanted to disappear.

"When you were her age," interrupted Abuelita Alpha, "you were chasing every boy *en el valle — sinvergüenza*. I will not have you teaching my granddaughters —"

"I was not chasing boys!" protested Trini. "Men were chasing me! And they are not YOUR granddaughters only!"

Just then a hand appeared, like divine intervention, and pulled Fabi to the back of the restaurant and into the restroom. As usual, it was her baby sister, Alexis, to the rescue!

Alexis slammed the bathroom door behind them and Fabiola sank down to the floor, covering her face with her hands. She wanted to dissolve into the pink tiled walls.

"Oh, my God! I can't believe that just happened. I can never show my face in there again. I hope there was no one from school there."

Alexis started to laugh. "Fabi, *estás loca*. What possessed you to buy tampons from our *Sunday school* teacher?"

"Hey, it's not funny!"

"No?" Alexis said, laughing even harder. She leaned against the wall for support as she held her stomach and wiped the tears from her eyes.

"Well, maybe a little." Fabiola tried to keep a straight face. She looked at her sister and couldn't help cracking up along with her. "Oh, please, stop," Fabi protested, applying pressure to the cramp on her left side from laughing so hard. "You're going to make me pee my pants."

"Well, there's the toilet," Alexis cried, doubling over in hysterics.

When the girls finally got control over their giggles, Fabi pulled herself up to wash her face. Her sister was running her fingers over her newly flatironed hair. Even though they were sisters by blood, they really looked nothing alike.

Grandma Trini said they were like different flowers from the same garden. Alexis got her light-colored skin and petite figure from their mother's Basque roots. Fabi's strong indigenous features and thick frame stemmed from her dad's family in Mexico. They were made from the same ingredients, but as different as mild and *picante* chili.

And Fabi didn't understand her sister's latest obsession with flat hair. Sure, everyone at the mall was doing it, but Alexis naturally had the most beautiful soft curls. Fabi would trade her plain hair for her sister's any day.

"Poor Mom," Alexis commented as she adjusted her sparkly silver headband.

"What do you mean?" Fabi asked. "I was the one crucified in there."

"Yeah, but Mom is the one who has to deal with them all day long," Alexis explained. "You should consider yourself lucky that you didn't have to sit through Grandma Trini's 'how to insert a tampon' workshop." The two sisters busted out laughing again.

"Hey, let's get out of here, go somewhere else for the afternoon," Fabi said.

"How? And where? I have to practice my

violin scales." Alexis peeked through the cracked door. "Besides, the wolves are still out there."

Fabiola thought for a second. "Okay, then." She looked up at the small window that led to the back alley — freedom. "Help me up here and we can climb out. Then we can go find some fun."

Grandpa Frank lived around the corner from the restaurant. He grew the sweetest watermelons in the Valley. The Garza girls were used to jumping the fence to grab whatever they wanted since his backyard grew an abundance of food this time of year. When Grandpa Frank had retired from the military, he made his living selling his fruit and vegetables at the *pulga* in Alton on Sundays. But these days he could hardly drive himself anywhere anymore, and there were always tons of stuff up for grabs in his garden.

The girls picked a couple of small, round watermelons and headed to the house of their aunt Consuelo, Santiago's mom. She lived a couple of blocks down in a new gated community with a sweet pool and a Jacuzzi. After locating the key, hidden under the aloe vera potted plant, they let themselves into their aunt's house. Alexis borrowed a sexy bikini while Fabi put on an old T-shirt and shorts. In just a few minutes they were cooling off in the pool, trying to out-cannonball each other splash for splash.

"Now this is how I should have spent my whole summer," Fabi lamented with a sigh, lifting herself out of the water to relax in a lounge chair.

Alexis appeared a few moments later and stretched out in the chair next to her sister. She closed her eyes as if going to sleep. "I can't believe I'm starting high school next week." She opened one eye and looked over. "Do you think people will like me?"

Fabi shot up. "What? Are you crazy? Of course they're going to like you. Just be yourself and people will *love* you." Alexis didn't look convinced. "Besides, lots of your friends from junior high will be there. And, you'll have me there, too. I'll take good care of you," Fabi added reassuringly.

"I don't know what I would do without you," Alexis said, reaching out to squeeze her hand. "You're the best sister in the world."

Fabi beamed with pride. She closed her eyes and soaked in the delicious warm rays of the sun. She heard her sister get up to go back in the water.

"Hey, wetbacks!" a boy's voice called out from behind them. Fabi opened her eyes and sat up, staring openmouthed at Alexis, who was just as shocked. Who was calling them wetbacks?

But before Fabi could find the source of the insult, there was a huge splash. Moments later, Fabi's sister was bobbing up from under the water, coughing and screeching. Before Fabi could say anything, two big, strong hands grabbed her and pulled her up and out of her chair.

It was Santiago — of course. *That jerk*, Fabi thought as he tried to push her into the pool. But Fabi reached out and held tightly to his forearms. They tumbled into the pool together with a big splash. Alexis screamed happily and jumped on Santiago's back, trying to dunk him. Fabi swam over and splashed water on her cousin, who was yelling, "I give up! I give up!"

It was a perfect ending to summer.

chapter 2

The day was sure to be a scorcher. It was only 7:30 in the morning and the Dos Rios High marquee said it was 85 degrees. Fabiola looked over at her younger sister, who was holding tightly to her new backpack, slung over her right shoulder, heavily loaded down with new school supplies.

"Don't worry," Fabi said, giving her sister's arm a squeeze. "I won't let anyone pick on you."

Alexis tried to smile, but she looked small and fragile beside the towering high school students. Fabi could easily remember what her own first day at Dos Rios High had been like — it was only last year that she'd been standing where her sister was now. The imposing new building with its grand marble dome, numerous palm trees, and pretty fountains seemed out of place in their small, dusty town. It reminded Fabi of a storybook oasis in *One Thousand and One Arabian Nights*. If it weren't for her best friend Georgia Rae having such a good sense of direction, they would have been lost all year. Fabi felt a touch of sadness. Georgia Rae was starting her first day at Mac High today. It was just thirty miles away, but it felt like the opposite side of the moon.

"Let me see your schedule," Fabi said to Alexis. She reviewed the list quickly. "Okay, you have Mrs. Lara for freshman English. She's real nice. Try to sit in the front of the room. That way she won't call on you as much. Eww, you have Mr. Goss for science," Fabi went on, making a gagging expression. "We used to call him Mr. Gross. He spits when he talks, so try to sit at the very back." Alexis's eyes widened in alarm. "It's not that big a deal. C'mon." Fabi started climbing the steps. "I'll walk you over."

Alexis sighed. "Thanks. I can't help being so nervous. Look at my hand." It was shaking. "I don't know what I would do without you — hey!" A short, gawky boy with long, sweeping bangs rushed right into her.

"Excuse you!" Fabi called out at him. The boy adjusted the stack of books he was carrying to pull out his earplugs. He smiled sheepishly, hip-hop music blasting from the tiny speakers, and mouthed "Sorry" before hurrying back down the hallway. Fabi rolled her eyes and shrugged her shoulders at Alexis. Then she looked back at the river of students streaming up and down the halls.

"The thing about high school," Fabi said, navigating her little sister expertly around a swarm of girls fixing their hair in a locker mir-ror, "is that there are rules — just like in the real world. Once you understand the rules, everything falls into place."

"Rules?" Alexis asked, looking everywhere in awe.

They were standing in the main hall that fed into five adjacent buildings. Hundreds of students pushed through the entrance-way. Fabi noted the new faces. Dos Rios High served all the small towns in the area by bus-ing the students in. The chatter of friends reunited after the summer was deafening. Fabiola scuffed her Vans at the emblem of the two catfish fighting each other etched into the linoleum floor. "See those beef-heads over there in the yellow and black matching jackets?" she asked her sister. The group of boys she was referring to were high-fiving and punching each other on the shoulders in some barbaric masculinity rite. "Those are the jocks. Big, burly, all into sports. Not much for personality, though."

Alexis smiled. "They're cute."

"Don't waste your time," Fabi said sternly. "Those guys only hang out with cheerleaders

[29]

or girls from the dance squad. Like I said, there are rules."

Fabi turned toward a crowd of gorgeous girls with perfect hair, manicured nails, and beautiful skin. They looked like they'd just stepped out of a fashion magazine, and reeked of money. "Those are the *fresas*, mostly rich kids from Mexico. They won't even look at you unless you're wearing the 'right' designer clothes. There are the popular kids who are all into student council, school spirit, and bake sales. In the computer lab and library you find the geeks and nerds. Then there are the emos, who wear all black with lots of black eyeliner." A girl with rainbow hair and a nose ring marched by in combat boots, just as Fabi added, "And the freaks. They come in all shapes and sizes."

"What are you?" Alexis asked, trying to figure out her place in this new world.

Fabi looked around. "I guess I'm normal."

"Normal?" Alexis laughed.

"Yeah." Fabi grinned. "Normal."

A group of familiar faces approached Fabi. "Who's this?" a girl with straight black hair and cute glasses asked. Alexis blushed and shrank back behind Fabi.

"Guys," Fabi announced, her voice full of pride, "you remember my little sister, Alexis. Alexis, these are my friends. This is Noelia, and Violet, and this is Mona."

"No way!" said Violet, practically shouting.

"You're so big! I mean, *older*," Mona said admiringly.

"And so pretty," added Noelia. "I love your hair."

Alexis played with her straightened locks and said, "Oh, this? You guys are just being nice. How much did my sister pay you to say those things to me?"

"Your sister," teased Mona, "never has money."

"She's worse than my grandma, who saves her money in an old shoe," added Noelia, giggling.

"Oh, you guys think you're sooo funny,"

Fabiola cut in. "Ha ha." She pushed her sister away from the group. "Watch out for those girls," she said loud enough for them to hear. "They're trouble."

"That's why you love us," Violet replied, throwing kisses in the air. "See ya!"

"Your friends are nice," Alexis said as they walked down the hall.

"Yeah, I guess, but don't flatter them."

Alexis smiled. "I'll try to remember that."

Fabi noticed Alexis staring across the hall and followed her gaze. She didn't like what she saw. Luckily, just then the bell rang. "C'mon, let's hurry," she told her sister, trying to pull her away.

"Who's that?" Alexis asked, not budging.

"I don't know. C'mon, let's hurry or you're going to be late."

"You're lying," Alexis said quietly. "I can tell when you're lying because you start blinking a lot."

"No, I don't." Fabi grabbed her sister by the elbow and dragged her down the hall.

"Yes, you do," Alexis giggled. "Oh, c'mon," she protested, trying to twist out of her sister's grip, looking over her shoulder. "This is high school, Fabi, and for the first time I don't know everybody. It's the greatest feeling. High school is supposed to be the best time of our lives." She stopped struggling and bit her lower lip. "I want to have fun. Do crazy things."

Fabi tried to reassure her sister. She didn't want to be overbearing. "You will do crazy things. I promise. But trust me on this: You don't want to do them with Dex."

Alexis's eyes lit up. "That's his name? Dex. Dex what? I thought you didn't know him."

"Dex Nada, because that boy is *nada* to you."

"You like him?" Alexis asked, her eyes growing cautious.

Fabiola tripped over her foot. "*Dex Andrews?* Oh, God, no."

"Great!" Alexis cheered.

"No, that's not what I meant."

"Then you do like him?"

"No, I mean I don't like him. Besides, he has a girlfriend. She's not very nice." Fabi stopped in front of a doorway and said, "Here's your homeroom." Alexis just stared back at her with a confused expression. "Listen," Fabi said with a sigh, "you've just got to trust me on this one. I'll explain at lunch, okay? I'll meet you by the main entrance." Then Fabi hurried away to her own classroom on the second floor.

Alexis watched her sister leave, lingering at the door for a moment. Then she quickly turned into the classroom to find a seat.

Fabi waited patiently by the main entrance as promised, but her sister never materialized. She stared down the hallway, wondering what could be keeping her. Lunch had started over twenty minutes ago. She wished Georgia Rae were here. Then they could split up and look for her. *Alexis is so small*, Fabi thought. She could be stuffed in a locker someplace or getting bullied in some corner of the mazelike building. Worry started to grow in her stomach. Maybe her sister had gone ahead to the cafeteria? Maybe she couldn't find the main entrance? Fabi couldn't stand to wait a moment longer and hurried down the hallway to the lunchroom.

The cafeteria was crammed with bodies. How was she supposed to find her sister in here? Every girl seemed to be wearing glittery headbands and have straightened brown hair. A high-pitched laugh made her turn around. It had come from a group of students hovering over the back corner table. Something pulled Fabi over for a closer look.

There, in the center of the table, speaking with animated flair, was her little sister. The people around her looked enraptured by whatever she was saying. Alexis seemed to be in her element — carefree, confident, and funny. It was such a stark contrast to the timid and shy kid Fabi had left that morning.

Alexis saw Fabi approach and waved her over. Fabi was glad her sister had made friends.

She'd known that Alexis had nothing to worry about. Fabi planned to tease her about it later.

But as Fabiola got closer, she noticed who Alexis was with, and flinched unconsciously. Now she wished she had warned her sister better about who to stay away from.

Alexis beamed with excitement. "Hey, Fabi, where have you been? Lunch is almost over," she said, without a care in the world. "I thought you were supposed to look after me," she joked. The crowd laughed with her.

Fabi felt an uncomfortable heat prick her ears. "I was waiting in the main entrance, where we agreed to meet."

Alexis guiltily raised her fingertips to her puckered lips. "Oops, that's right. My bad. Well, it is my first day," she said, more to the group sitting with her than to Fabi. "Hey, come sit with us," she added, scooting a boy over so her sister could squeeze in. Fabi looked at the space her sister made for her and knew she wouldn't fit, but she didn't want to admit that. The popular kids in their matching Hollister outfits waited to see what Fabi would do. She could feel their eyes assessing her wardrobe. Although there was a dress code at Dos Rios High, it was rarely enforced. Fabi didn't care much for clothes — just give her a comfortable pair of jeans and her Vans and she was happy. The popular kids stared at her like she had two heads.

"It's okay," Fabi said, growing flustered. "I forgot that I promised Ms. Muñoz to stop by her class at lunch."

"Fa-bi," Alexis said in an irritated voice.

"It's cool, really." She tried to smile, pretending that all was good. "I just wanted to make sure you were okay. And you are. So I should go." Fabi turned and hurried out of the cafeteria.

She stood in the hallway. Her heart felt heavy, but she didn't want to think about it. Not here. Not where anyone could see her. She let her feet guide her up to the second floor, past the library and science rooms. She just wanted to be alone.

This was not how she envisioned Alexis's first day at school. Alexis was *her* sister. Fabi wanted to be the one to introduce her to people and share her first experiences. Now she felt crushed. It was like the day she'd found out that Santa was actually her uncle Chunky in a red suit. Fabi wanted to cry, but that was just stupid. She couldn't keep Alexis to herself like some toy.

And then she stopped suddenly at the sound of loud smacking lips. It was coming from around the corner.

"Please don't do that," a guy's voice said.

"Oh, baby, I missed you so much," whined the girl. "Didn't you get my texts?"

"I got them." The guy's voice was cold and dry. "I got your calls, e-mails, and notes, too."

Fabiola jerked back against the wall. She wanted to run the other way. But she was paralyzed when she heard something loud smash the lockers.

"Damn it, Dex," the girl growled. "Don't make me mad. You don't want to see me mad.

You're acting ridiculous. Just give me another chance."

"Get off me," Dex stammered. "This is not working. I already told you. I need some space."

"Please don't do this!" the girl cried. Her voice cracked as if she was about to sob. "Please don't. You want space? I'll give you space! I'll do anything you want. Just please don't leave me. I need you. I love you."

"Stop! Stop this right now."

Fabi heard shuffling steps.

"No way!" the guy said. "Take your hands off me. You're acting crazy!" Then Dex Andrews came around the corner in a half sprint. Fabi recognized his tall athletic frame. But just in case she hadn't, he'd had his name shaved into the back of his hair like a tattoo design. Dex was determined to get out of there quick, which was a good thing for Fabi, who was standing flat against a doorway.

"Dex!" cried Melodee Stanton, following him around the corner. But Dex was gone. Melodee stood there, sniffling. Her black mascara was running down her cheeks. "I thought I smelled menudo," she said in a cold, evil voice. Melodee stared at Fabiola with her gray eyes, which she always covered with tons of smoky eye shadow. "Did you enjoy the show?"

Fabi tried to think of something quick. "I'm sorry. I was just walking and I didn't mean to . . ."

"Didn't mean to what?" snapped Melodee, trying to pull herself together. "Didn't mean to be a stupid loser? But you are!" Melodee wiped her cheek and then combed her fingers through her layered blonde hair. "You better not tell anyone about what you just heard. You got it, Fatty?"

Fabi wanted to correct her. Ever since that stupid AmeriCorps teacher from New York mispronounced her nickname as "Fatty," everyone, especially Dex Andrews and his friends, thought it was so hilarious to call her that. She had hoped that people would mature over the summer break, but obviously some hadn't.

Melodee stepped right up to Fabi's face and

sneered in a dead serious voice, "If I hear that you're talking behind my back, I will get you. I will get you so bad. You'll wish you were never born. Got it?"

Fabi nodded, trying not to breathe.

"Fine." Melodee smiled smugly. "And can you do the whole school a favor and buy some new clothes?" she added with a cruel laugh. "Later, loser."

Fabiola listened to Melodee's footsteps echo down the hall. She wished for the courage to break that little witch in two like a twig. This was a perfect example of why there were rules in school. She had violated the most important one: Don't wander the halls alone.

If only Georgia Rae hadn't moved. If only *Fabi* lived someplace else, somewhere far, *far* away. But wishing never got her anywhere.

The lunchtime bell sounded, interrupting her pitiful thoughts. Fabi sighed and gathered what was left of her self-respect and headed to the library.

After school, Santiago was leaning against the hood of his black truck in the Dos Rios High parking lot. Fabi raced up to him and gave him a great big hug. She hadn't realized how badly she needed to see a friendly face.

"Hey, *guapa*," Santiago said, hugging her back. "You okay?"

Fabi smiled, trying not to show too much emotion. "I'm just glad to see you." Santiago and her dad were the only ones who called her "*guapa*." It was actually kind of embarrassing, since no one but her family thought she was pretty.

"So how was your first day? Where's Alexis?"

Fabi opened her mouth to tell him about her new art teacher, but just then Alexis appeared from nowhere and jumped on Santiago's back.

"Hey, Santi," she said, grinning and hugging his neck. Alexis was literally bouncing with a radiant glow as her cousin lowered her to the ground. "Oh, high school is so much *fun*," she went on. "I met so many cool people and they all wanted me to be their friend and they all wanted to sit with me at lunch. And you should see the mariachi group here on campus. They are so professional and they wear all-white outfits with green bows and red sashes. I told them I played violin and they want me to try out, but I also signed up for cheerleading and drama. Did you know that they do musicals here? And there's just so much to do I don't know how I'll find time to do homework! Oh, my, I need to practice. I can't wait to tell my voice teacher."

"I didn't see you at school today," Fabiola said to Santiago when Alexis finally paused to take a breath.

Santiago smiled, knowing he'd been caught. "Well, you know, I was going to come. After I dropped you two off and everything, I realized that I forgot this book I was supposed to turn in last year and when I got home —"

"Heads up!" someone called out.

Fabi looked up to see a football coming

straight at her. Alexis screamed. Fabi raised her arm, ready to block the hit. But then a big, beefy shoulder banged into her, shoving her back, hard.

"Sorry 'bout that," Dex Andrews said, attempting to help Fabi but all along staring at Alexis. He'd caught the football, of course, and was now casually tossing it in his hands as if nothing had happened.

Alexis was practically drooling like a love-sick puppy. "Oh, thank you so much for saving my sister from that horrible ball. I don't know what we would've done if you hadn't been here!"

"Yeah" — Dex smiled — "my boy has terrible aim." He gestured to a pack of jocks laughing and making hooting noises twenty feet away.

"No, he doesn't," Fabi yelled, pissed. "You did that on purpose."

Dex turned to Fabi with a fake-worried expression. "Why would I do something like that? And to you?"

Santiago squeezed Fabi's arm and stepped in between her and Dex.

"'Cause you're a punk and that's what punks do," he said.

Dex straightened up, sizing up Santiago. He was a foot taller and at least fifty pounds heavier, but that didn't intimidate Santiago one bit.

"Santiago Reyes!" Mr. Castillo, the vice principal and ex–high school football star, called out from the top of the stairway. All the students around them stopped and stared. "I heard you had the flu today."

"I did," Santiago said, his feet grounded firmly and his voice defiant. "But then I got better."

Mr. Castillo obviously didn't believe him, but he let it slide. "Excellent, then I will expect you in my office first thing tomorrow morning."

Santiago squinted his eyes tight just for a second. He did that whenever he was really mad and trying to control his temper. "Yes, sir," he said, still holding his face up to Dex.

The vice principal looked at Dex and then at Santiago again. "All right, you boys need to go. *Now!*"

"Yes, Mr. Castillo," Dex answered, turning to leave. But before he did he turned back to Santiago and said, "I'll see you around, *bro.*"

Santiago snapped, "I'm right here, *baby*, whenever you're ready."

"Fabiola!" the vice principal called out.

"Yes, sir?"

"Get your cousin out of here. Right now."

Fabi pulled Santiago away.

"I'm leaving already," Santiago shouted, climbing into his truck. The girls scrambled in after him as Santiago angrily turned up the volume on the radio and peeled out of the school parking lot.

"I hate Mr. Castillo," Santiago raved. "He's always trying to talk to me like he's my dad or something." He stared straight ahead, lost in his thoughts for a moment. "He's just trying to score points with my mom."

Fabi and Alexis said nothing on the trip home. This could not be a good start to the new school year.

chapter 3

Sunday was menudo day. Customers, young and old, came to Garza's after church for a bowl of Leonardo's tripe stew. Some claimed that it had magical properties — the ability to revive the soul, soften tempers, and cure a wicked hangover.

That Sunday after the first week back at school, Fabiola was busy busing tables, taking new orders, and topping coffee cups. Her sister was sitting with her grandmother Alpha, whispering. There was a stack of schoolbooks to her right, but Alexis was interested only in the latest gossip. Across the room, Grandma Trini was dusting the Little Rafa shrine with loving care as she softly sang an old love song, *"Un viejo amor, dadadidadadadida."*

"Time for another fill-up," Grandpa Frank called out, waving his empty cup in the air.

"Yes, sir," Fabi replied while carrying a bucket heavy with dirty plates to the back, where Chuy, her dad's assistant/right-hand man, was busy loading the dishwasher.

"How's it going, Chuy?" Fabi asked slowly. Jesus "Chuy" Mendez was born in Eagle Pass to a Mexican man and a Kickapoo Indian woman. But he was born at home and his father had taken him to Mexico, so he didn't have any birth records. Now back in Texas, Chuy was taking English classes in the evenings and looking for his mother on weekends. He liked to practice his English with Fabi because she never made fun of his accent.

"Many of customers to . . . day." Chuy nodded as a couple walked in, setting off the door

chime. Magda showed them to a clean table by the door and motioned for Fabi to wait on them.

"Good morning," Fabiola greeted the elderly couple as she approached, pulling out her order book from her back pocket. "Welcome to Garza's. Can I take your order?"

The woman with fine, short white hair smiled, looking a tad embarrassed as she glanced at both sides of the menu. "I'm sorry, but we're vegan," she said in an East Coast accent. "We don't eat things made from animal products. How are your beans cooked?"

Fabi's eyes lit up. "Vegan? I've heard of that. That's cool. I'm a vegetarian."

The woman looked happily surprised.

"Really, I am," Fabi assured her. "And I'll be honest with you, most of our food is cooked with pork fat. But I can ask my dad to put together a veggie fajita plate or rolled potato and zucchini tacos, grilled in a little olive oil and topped with fresh shredded lettuce and diced tomatoes, green onions, and jalapeños?"

The man laughed. "That would be great. We actually didn't know what we were going to eat. Everything we've seen so far is big on meat and cheese."

"Welcome to the Rio Grande Valley," Fabi said, rolling her eyes in a friendly way. "I'll be right back with your water."

The door chimed again and Santiago stood at the entrance, waiting to be noticed. In a matter of seconds Grandma Trini was screaming and rushing over, covering him with kisses.

"Ay, *mi* baby. What a miracle. Look at you. You finally show up. Where have you been? You been working out, *mijo*?" She squeezed his arms. "You look like you've been working out. You hungry? What do you want?" Trini turned to the kitchen and shouted for Chuy.

Santiago jumped onto the stool next to Grandpa Frank. He gently slapped him on the back. "How's it going, Grandpa? How's the coffee?"

Grandpa Frank smiled, revealing his gold

tooth as it shined brightly. "Delicious." Alexis and Abuelita Alpha joined them. Santiago's magnetic charm drew people to him like ships to a beacon on a stormy night.

Fabi headed to the kitchen. Her dad was mixing a pot of chili. His lunch was in the corner — untouched. "Hey, Pa, I have a couple here that wants vegan food. I thought we could . . ."

"Be-*what*?" her dad asked, annoyed. Customers rarely made special requests or complained. The menu at Garza's hadn't changed in twenty years. Her father saw no reason to tinker with what worked. "What's that?"

"Remember how I was telling you that I'm a vegetarian now and I don't eat any animals?"

Her dad sighed, moving sluggishly around the kitchen. Fabi noticed the dark bags under his eyes and wished for the millionth time that her dad would take some time off. *Ha! You can rest when you're dead*, he always said.

Mr. Garza came over to Fabi. The familiar warming scents of cinnamon and chili powder drifted into her nose as he put his hand on her shoulder and leaned in so no one would hear. "I don't know why you keep on with this diet stuff. I think you're fine. . . ."

Fabi pulled back. "It's not about diet stuff. I just want to be healthy, okay?"

"You don't think menudo is healthy? Look at me," he said, and pounded his wide chest. "I eat my food every day and I'm strong like a bull."

"Dad, it's not that," Fabi protested, but she knew she was wasting her breath. Her dad was not going to listen. No one in her family ever listened.

"You tell those *be-ganes*," he declared, his voice getting louder, "that if they don't like our food, they can take their business someplace else!" And with that, Leonardo Garza turned and dropped a heavy skillet on the industrial-sized stove with a loud clang.

"But, Dad," Fabi pleaded softly.

"Go tell them!" he shouted, motioning for her to get out of *his* kitchen.

Frustrated, Fabiola went back to the customers and apologized. It was always the same thing with her dad. Every time Fabi tried to suggest something new to add to the menu — ways to attract different kinds of customers — he always shot her down. The couple was nice and left quietly. She watched them go, but was soon interrupted by her cousin.

"Hey," Santiago complained from the counter, "I didn't order this." Chuy emerged from the kitchen wiping his hands. "I said I wanted chicken, not cheese enchiladas."

Chuy pressed his lips together nervously. Then he said, "No, you say cheese," in his halted, broken English.

"You calling me a liar?" Santiago snapped. "You can't even speak English right. I don't know why you even work here!" He pushed the plate away as if it were something disgusting like roadkill.

"That is quite enough, Santiago," Magda ordered sternly from behind the register.

Although Fabi's dad was the king of the kitchen, the rest of the restaurant was under her mother's control. When she gave an order, everyone jumped — even some of the local customers. No one wanted to get on her bad side.

"Aw, Tía," Santiago said, acting like nothing had happened. "I was just messing with him. You know how much I like this border brother."

"Chuy is a hard worker," Magda stated, putting her strong arms on her hips. "He works six days a week alongside your uncle and goes to school in the evenings. When are *you* going to come in and start working for all the food you eat?"

"Aw, Tía," Santiago cooed again. "You know I'm going to do it. I love you guys. You're my family. I'll come in. I promise. I just need to take my car into the shop. Then I thought maybe we could all drive down to the island for the afternoon."

"Santiago," Magda scolded, but there was no anger behind it. "You know I can't take time off from the restaurant."

"But even God took a day of rest," Santiago urged innocently. Then he turned and called over his shoulder, "Isn't that right, Chuy?"

Magda shook her head. "Oh, I can't stay mad at you. Just get your food and go fix that dumb car of yours," she said, shooing him away.

A car honked outside. "There's my ride," Santiago said.

"Who's that?" asked Abuelita Alpha, peeping out the window.

"Oh, it's just some friends," Santiago said, sliding the enchiladas into a Styrofoam box.

"Friends!" Alpha said, surprised. "Isn't that Victorino Salinas's kid?"

Grandma Trini rushed to the door as Santiago was trying to leave. "What are you doing with the Salinas brothers?" she cried.

"Grandma," Santiago tried to explain, "it's not what you think."

"No?" Trini exclaimed. "Really? How do you know what I'm thinking?"

"They're just giving me a ride, okay?"

"Not in that car. Not with those people. *Con esa gente no se juega*," Trini protested.

Alpha made the sign of the cross. "That's the devil's car."

Santiago laughed. "Oh, come on, you two. I promise it's nothing like that. I just need a ride to the mechanic. If you want, I can call you when I get there, all right?"

The two old ladies weren't convinced. Alpha was praying the rosary silently with her eyes closed as Trini blessed Santiago with the sign of the cross on his forehead. When he'd finally managed to break free from the grandmothers, Alexis and Fabiola followed their cousin out the door and watched him hop into the black Cadillac Escalade with tinted windows. On the back window was a picture of a skeletal figure draped in a long robe and holding a scythe.

Alexis's breath caught. She turned to Fabiola with a scared look on her face.

"*La Santa Muerte*," Fabi whispered. Saint Death.

Inside the restaurant, there was a charged buzz, as if someone had kicked a hornets' nest. Locals were comparing rumors. Rudy, the used-car salesman, claimed that the Salinas brothers must be working with the drug dealers across the river if they were praying to *La Santa Muerte*, patron saint of drug dealers, prostitutes, and thieves. Liza Anzaldua, Fabi's older cousin, claimed it was all the marijuana they smoked that was making them crazy. Uncle Tito thought it might be a resurgence of Aztec culture in the new generation. But Abuelita Alpha was the most vocal and declared that *La Santa Muerte* was a devil-worshiping cult, and it had to be stopped!

Cherrio, an old friend of Grandpa Frank's, said, "What are you going to do, Alpha, take on *la mafia*? That's who's spreading that stuff, you know."

"Well, I know the first thing I'm going to do," Grandma Alpha replied, frustrated. "I'm going to church to pray. And if you are smart you'll go, too, Cherrio." She shook her pale, wrinkly finger at him. "Lord knows the last time you went to confession."

The old man shooed her off. Grandma Alpha was always scolding people for not going to church. Cherrio turned away from her and grumbled loudly into his cup, "Who made you Mother Superior?!"

Everyone started to laugh. The mood had lightened a little. Grandma Trini leaned in to Alexis and asked her to sing one of Little Rafa's romantic ballads. Alexis smiled as she danced her way to the jukebox and punched B-14. The high-pitched tones of an accordion melody erupted from the machine. Alexis hooked a microphone to the box and started to sway side to side in rhythm with the country beat. It was Fabiola's favorite song, "Cowboy Kisses in the Night."

Then Fabi's jaw dropped. She couldn't believe it. Her dad slowly walked out of the kitchen, took off his apron, and handed it to Chuy. He never left the kitchen! Leonardo ran his fingers through his hair as he crossed the room and reached his hand out for his wife. Magda met his eyes and smiled shyly, like a school-girl, and followed him toward the makeshift dance floor — the space cleared when a couple of tables were pushed to the side. Leonardo and Magda glided effortlessly across the floor — they didn't have to look at their feet or anything. The door chimed open. But Fabi, like everyone else in the restaurant, was so mesmerized by the dancing that she couldn't take her eyes off them. Fabi loved to watch her parents dance. It made her heart want to burst with pride. She noticed Alexis grinning from across the room. Their parents were still so in love after so many years.

As the crowd whooped and cheered for more, Fabi turned to see if anyone needed any-thing. And that's when she saw Dex Andrews standing by the door. What was he doing here? Fabi's mom made a shushing sound to grab her attention. Even though her mother was in the middle of the dance floor, she still ran the restaurant with a stick. Magda gestured for her to go see what he wanted, and there was no arguing with her mom.

Dex stared at Alexis as she began to sing a new song, an upbeat *conjunto* classic. There was a strange look in his eyes. Fabi didn't like it. She didn't like *him*, and especially didn't like him coming to her family's restaurant.

Fabi marched to the table where Dex had taken a seat. "What do you want?" she snapped.

Dex smirked. "How 'bout we start with a menu?"

"Oh, come on, what are you doing here? We both know you don't want to eat here."

"You don't know that," Dex snapped back.

"Are you trying to tell me that in all the years we've known each other, you never once came to my family's restaurant, but now, all of a sudden, you have an urge for our food?"

"Maybe I never had a reason to come before," Dex said, winking at Fabi.

So his reason now was her sister, Alexis? Oh, please! Fabi felt nauseous. "Well, we don't have menus. Actually, we're all out of food. Sorry." She smiled back so hard her cheeks hurt.

"Oh, Fabi," interrupted Grandma Trini, coming up behind her, "why are you acting so *maleducada*, and to such a handsome young man?" Trini pressed her chest forward. "And look at his letterman jacket." She hit Fabi playfully on the arm. "He's athletic. You like athletic boys, don't you, Fabi?" Trini smiled brightly at Dex and purred, "You should really try the chili con carne. It's real hot and spicy. You like hot and spicy?"

Dex started to squirm, and his face was turning bright red. Maybe Grandma Trini was not so embarrassing after all, Fabi thought with a smirk.

"I'll be right back with your order," Fabi said, and quickly walked away, leaving Dex alone with her cougar grandmother.

When Fabi returned a few minutes later,

she found Alexis sitting across from Dex at the table. Alexis was laughing in that high, fake, hair-tossing way that she did whenever she was trying too hard. The whole scene made Fabi sick, but what could she do?

"Here's your order," Fabi spat as she tossed a bowl of chili on the table, spilling some of the meaty broth.

"Okay," Dex said, a little annoyed, "thanks."

Alexis shot her a "go away" look. The betrayal was sharp, like a knife in her back. Fabi couldn't believe how her sister was acting — especially after Fabi had explained the rules to her that week at school! As she stalked off, Fabi overheard Dex say, "What's your sister's problem?" It took all of Fabi's strength to keep walking away.

Dex left thirty minutes later, but Fabi was forced to listen to her sister retell the entire conversation. Thankfully, in the middle of Alexis's long description, the door chimed again. Fabi looked up — and instantly regretted it. Melodee

Stanton was standing at the door, carrying a Louis Vuitton purse and an ugly rat-looking dog in a matching sweater. What was going *on*? This was way too much drama for one day. Maybe it wasn't too late to change schools.

"Hey," Fabi said, meeting Melodee at the door.

Melodee jumped at the sight of Fabi. She gave the place a quick once-over. "You work here?" she asked in disbelief.

"Yes, this is my family's restaurant." Fabi extended her arm out in a sweeping gesture. "I've been working here since I was seven years old. But I don't think you came to hear my life story."

Melodee huffed, glancing at her Gucci watch in annoyance. "No, I don't have time to chat. All I want to know is if Dex was here." She looked over Fabi's shoulder and into the kitchen. Did she think Dex was hiding under the counter?

"You just missed him," Fabi replied, pointing to the door behind Melodee. "He went that way."

Melodee turned to go, but stopped and looked Fabi in the eye. "What did he want?"

Just then Alexis came out of the bathroom. She grabbed a bottle of Coke and returned to her table to begin her homework. Melodee followed Fabi's gaze.

"I don't know," Fabi said. "I think he likes his chili con carne hot and spicy."

Melodee made a foul face, or maybe it was just the way she caked on her makeup. Fabi always wondered how she kept it from melting off her face in the humidity. "Oh, you think you're so clever, Miss Fabiola Garza, don't you?"

"Are you stalking Dex, or something?"

Melodee turned pale. "No, I'm not. I'm just —" she stumbled as she started to grow flustered. "I just need to talk to him, okay? And it's none of your business anyway, and I don't know why I'm even explaining myself to you." Melodee turned quickly and marched out the door, leaving a trail of perfume behind her that rivaled Grandma Trini's.

Fabi rushed to the bathroom and locked herself in a stall, trying to calm her thumping heart. She didn't know why this was happening to her. Dex and Melodee, both in one day! What were the chances? She didn't know why they bugged her so much. Sure, Dex was a jock, a jerk, and he had picked on her all freshman year. And Melodee was a pill — one of those big fat vitamin pills that make you gag. And now with Alexis gaga for Dex, what was she supposed to do?

Fabi pulled out her cell phone and sent a text to her best friend. There were only two words:

Rescue me.

chapter 4

The following Friday, Georgia Rae picked Fabi up after school. They were going to the Dos Rios football game later that evening, but first Fabi wanted to see Georgia Rae's new place. The tiny apartment was cramped with piles of unopened boxes stacked to the ceiling. Georgia Rae used to live on a large cattle ranch that her great-great-grandfather built, filled with animals like quail, hogs, and turkeys running wild in the hills. But when her mom's boyfriend got caught for smuggling, they had to move into an apartment complex in McAllen.

"What did your mom do with all the animal taxidermy?" Fabi asked. The rest of Georgia Rae's family were avid hunters and always mounted their prized kills, mostly whitetail bucks, ducks, and bobcats. It was a little creepy at night when the light sparkled on their glass eyes.

"Mom's gotten rid of everything. She's on this kick about how we have to start over," Georgia Rae said, looking bored as she covered her short brown bob with a mist of hair spray. She glanced around her bedroom and shrugged. "It's a lot smaller than the ranch, but my mom's actually way happier in the city. Did I tell you about the theater department at my school?" she asked, suddenly switching subjects. "My drama teacher says I have a lot of potential. She said I should try out for the lead in the new play. Can you believe it? You should see where all the drama students hang out. You're totally going to love it. They have vegetarian food there, too." She grabbed her keys from her dresser. "C'mon, let's go."

Georgia Rae took Fabi to a cute green wooden house that had been converted into a coffee shop, with cool paintings and old record covers decorating the walls. The new, hip place was so funky and surreal, it felt out of place in the Valley — it belonged in a bigger city like Austin or Houston.

Fabi smiled. "You are so lucky to live here." She instantly felt twenty times cooler sitting on an animal-print lounge sofa and sipping on a caramel macchiato. This was how civilized people should live, Fabi thought as she grinned to herself — with movie theaters, a mall, art galleries. "If I lived here I would spend all my time drinking caramel macchiatos."

"I know, huh?" Georgia Rae smiled brightly, enjoying the opportunity to show off this new place to her friend. "I just can't believe that your parents gave you Friday night off."

"Actually, Chuy is covering for me. He's going to lock up the restaurant tonight." Fabiola hugged her best friend tightly and cried to her in distress. "I've missed you so much! I can't believe you deserted me. School sucks without you. Do you think your mom would adopt me?"

"Oh, c'mon," Georgia Rae kidded, pushing Fabi back on the couch. "It can't be that bad."

"It's worse," Fabi said. "It's like a nightmare that I can't wake up from. My own baby sister has become one of the popular girls."

"No!" Georgia Rae cried, in a suitably horrified tone.

"I swear, it's the worst!" But Fabi couldn't hold back the giggles. "Seriously, though, I was really excited about her starting high school. I had BIG plans for us this year. But now . . . I feel like her sad, needy sister."

Georgia Rae reached over and squeezed Fabi's hand.

"I'm okay," she tried to reassure her friend. "It's just strange now. I don't know how to act around her anymore. And Dex Andrews is all into her."

Georgia Rae stuck her index finger in her mouth as if wanting to gag. It made Fabi laugh again.

"I know, gross, huh? And there's no talking sense to Alexis. She's so enamored with high school, and it makes me feel like a pathetic wet blanket."

"You have nothing to feel pathetic about," Georgia Rae said, slapping her palm on the table. "All those guys are super lame-o's. Besides, what happened to our plan?"

"Yeah, but you moved away. You left me," Fabi lamented. "And you have all this now."

"You still have your quinceañera money?"

"Yeah, it's all still there. In the bank, just like we talked about." It was Georgia Rae's idea that Fabiola should skip the traditional quinceañera party in exchange for a trip to New York City. Her aunt Consuelo had already agreed to take them.

"Then what are you complaining about? In a couple of years we'll be out of here. No more burning sun or dust devils. No more dumb jocks and prissy dance-squad girls. College is a whole new world. We just got to get there."

"Oh, Georgia Rae," Fabi wailed, wanting to cry. "You're so right. I can't tell you how much I needed to see you. You always know exactly what to say. I'm going to have to come visit you once a week — to keep me from going crazy."

"Yes, you will. Now, enough of this sad talk." She glanced at her watch. "We better hurry. We don't want to be late to the first game of the season."

On the drive back to Dos Rios, Fabi's stomach started to somersault. She looked over her shoulder at the road behind her as Georgia Rae drove. They were leaving behind department stores and five-star restaurants for dry country landscape, wild sunflowers, and roadkill. Fabi held her breath as they crossed the city limits. Despite her reservations, and despite their feelings about most of the jocks at school, Fabi and Georgia Rae always went to the Dos Rios football games. They loved to watch their team kick butt on the field.

"Hey," Georgia Rae said, pointing out the truck window, "isn't that that new boy, what's-his-name?"

"Milo, I think," Fabi said.

On the side of the road, looking stranded, stood Hermilo Castillo-Collins. Next to him, steam was shooting from the hood of an old BMW sedan like a busted fire hydrant. Georgia Rae pulled her truck over and parked it on the shoulder to see if he needed some help.

Milo had moved to the Valley from Phoenix, Arizona, toward the end of last year. Fabiola didn't know him very well because he stayed to himself a lot. The jocks teased him because of his funny clothes.

"You look like you need help," Georgia Rae said, hopping out of her white Toyota pickup.

"Hey, don't I know you?" Milo asked Fabi.

"Yeah," Fabi said, growing shy. She was

always self-conscious around new people. "I sit behind you in Geometry."

"That's right." He nodded, smiling.

Georgia Rae looked under his hood. "What seems to be the problem here?"

Milo blushed and said, "I have no idea. This piece-of-junk car is always breaking down on me. It started to smell, and then white smoke started coming out of the hood. That can't be good, right? I'm glad you guys stopped. I didn't want to leave my car because of all my equipment."

"Looks like you have a leaking radiator," Fabi said, pointing to the wet spot on the ground. "Or it could be the coolant hose. Check the antifreeze level to make sure it's not low."

"Dude, you have *no* antifreeze," Georgia Rae said in disbelief.

Milo shrugged his shoulders, looking uncomfortable. "I told you I didn't know nothing about cars." He leaned over and peeked at the motor. "Are all the girls around here professional mechanics, or are you two special?"

"Fabi's the car whiz." Georgia Rae motioned to her friend with a nod.

"Well, I do have eight uncles on my dad's side," she explained. "You hang out with them long enough and you, too, can become an expert on cars, football, and grilling carne asada."

Milo chuckled softly. He had a disarming smile. Fabi and Georgia Rae peered into the backseat of the old BMW. There were milk crates stuffed with audio equipment and electrical cords.

"Well, we're on our way to the football game. But if you want, we can put your stuff in the back of my truck and give you a ride into town," Georgia Rae suggested.

"I'm sure my dad has some antifreeze lying around," Fabi said.

"You'd do that?" Milo asked, surprised. "Thanks."

The girls helped him lug his turntables, mixer gizmos, and crates of vinyl records into the truck. As they pulled back onto the highway,

Milo put in one of his mix CDs for them. The music was really nice, full of soft hip-hop dance beats. Milo closed his eyes and nodded his head when he listened to the music, as if he were in some kind of trance. Fabi closed her eyes and tried to dissolve into the music, too, but after a moment, she opened her eyes again, feeling stupid. There was a thin smile on Milo's face. He was watching her. Fabi turned quickly and stared out the window.

The sun had already set when they stopped in front of her family's restaurant. "Hey, do you want to come in?" she asked, opening the passenger door. "We'll be quick. I know just where my dad keeps the antifreeze."

Milo and Georgia Rae followed Fabi into the restaurant. She planned to be in and out of there in less than five minutes.

But as soon as she stepped inside, Fabi stopped in her tracks.

Chuy was lying on the floor. Bruises covered his face. Alexis was cradling his head in her lap while her mother was carefully trying to clean his wounds. Chuy's right eye was swollen shut and he was bleeding from his nose and a cut on his cheek. His shirt was ripped and there was a muddy boot print on his apron.

"What happened?!" Fabi cried, running over to Chuy.

Magda looked up at her with swollen eyes. "Oh, honey, I didn't call you because I didn't want you to worry."

"Mom, what is going on?"

Chuy tried to sit up. He opened his mouth as if to talk, but only bubbles of blood spouted from his busted lips.

"Don't move," Magda scolded as if he were a rude child not following instructions — but there was no anger behind it. "Your dad went to find your cousin," she said to Fabi.

"Mom, we should take him to the hospital. He's bleeding all over the floor."

Tears welled up in Magda's eyes. "We tried to . . . but Chuy wouldn't let us. He refuses to go to the hospital. He says it'll cost too much money."

"He could die!"

"Your cousin Benny is coming."

"But, Mom, he's only a dental hygienist," Fabi pointed out.

"That's even better. He'll clean him up real good now." Mrs. Garza looked up and added, "Georgia Rae, honey, go warm some fresh water." Fabiola had completely forgotten her friends standing next to her. "I'm glad you brought help," her mom told her. "We could use extra hands."

"Oh, yeah, this is Hermilo," Fabi said with a quick gesture. He waved shyly from the doorway.

"Come on in," Magda said, and nodded. "Now, in the bathroom down that hallway you'll find some fresh towels. Bring all of them."

Milo jumped. "Yes, ma'am." He followed her directions and hurried to the bathroom.

Alexis brushed Chuy's hair back with her

fingertips. "We were on our way to the football game and stopped by. The door was open and we just found him like this on the floor." Tears began to roll down her cheeks. "Who would do something like this? It makes no sense."

Fabi could only shake her head in disbelief. Who *would* do something like this? And at Garza's, of all places?

chapter 5

Later that night a boisterous crowd pushed at the door to the restaurant, but Fabi's mom told them Garza's was closed. From their elated cheers, Fabi gathered that the home team had won the football game. Alexis watched the crowd with longing eyes as her mother turned on the neon "Closed" sign.

Their cousin Benny had dropped out of the medical program at the University of Texas a couple classes shy of his degree. He knew enough to check Chuy's vitals and clean up his bloody face. By then, the rest of the family had arrived — both grandmas, Grandpa Frank, and Santiago's mom, Consuelo. Leo and Grandpa Frank had helped Chuy up to a chair as Milo and Fabiola mopped the dirty floor.

"Tell us who did this to you," Abuelita Alpha demanded over and over, shaking a fist of rosary beads so tight it was making her veined hand turn blue.

"Don't make him talk," scolded Magda. "He's just been assaulted."

"But we have to know who did it," Grandma Trini protested. She was wearing a tight Dos Rios High School T-shirt and still holding her pom-poms from the football game.

Chuy tried to speak but he was having trouble taking a deep breath.

"Are you sure his ribs aren't broken?" Fabi asked, leaning on the mop. "I still think we should go to the hospital."

Benny straightened up and dried his hands on a warm cloth. "He'll be fine. He's just a bit shaken up. Just needs some rest."

Chuy tried to sit up higher in his chair, and struggled to speak.

"He's trying to tell us something," Alexis said excitedly.

"He knows who did it!" Trini cried. "He knows who did it!"

With much effort, Chuy explained what had happened — how he had been locking up after his shift and hadn't been paying attention because he was in a hurry to get to the Western Union before it closed. Every payday, Chuy sent money home to Mexico to help support his father and siblings. Chuy's money put food on his family's table.

Then someone grabbed him from behind and someone else punched him in the stomach. He couldn't see their faces because it was dark. They took all his money and then beat him some more and threatened to kill him if he said anything or followed them.

It was a horrible story. No one wanted to admit that something like this could happen in tiny Dos Rios. This was not the big city like Houston or Reynosa — everyone knew everyone here, so they probably knew whoever had done this awful thing, too.

Fabi had always felt safe in Dos Rios. She used to walk around town at any hour of the night without a care. She knew every street and corner. But now, in a matter of minutes, she felt like a stranger in her own town. There were a lot of new faces, mostly refugees from the drug wars on the other side of the river. For the first time, Fabi realized, she was really afraid.

Leo and Benny helped Chuy move slowly out to Benny's SUV. A few minutes later they heard the engine grumble, taking Chuy home. Georgia Rae and Milo left moments later.

"*La Santa Muerte,*" Abuelita Alpha said in a soft voice. She made the sign of the cross over her face. "This place carries the stain. . . ." she muttered, looking around the restaurant as if the devil himself were going to pop up from under the table. "We must get Father Benavides to come bless the place at once."

Grandma Trini started to giggle softly behind her hand. "*Comadre*, now I know you're going senile. You can't blame the *diablo* for everything."

Abuelita Alpha turned bright red. "Don't mock the devil!"

But Grandma Trini only laughed louder, tossing her hair-sprayed, stiff *copete* back like a mane.

The door chimed, and Santiago walked in with a light step. "Hey, everybody, what's good to eat?" He stopped, noticing the somber mood. "Who died?"

"Santiago." Abuelita Alpha ran up to him before anyone could stop her. "You should not be walking around by yourself at night. It's not safe."

"Ah, Abuelita Alpha." Santiago snuck in a kiss on her cheek. "No one messes with me. Not with these guns," he said, flexing his arm muscles. Santiago went around the table kissing everyone. When he reached his mother, Consuelo, he threw a roll of dollar bills onto the table in front of her. "Ma, this is for you." Everyone gasped in surprise.

"What's this?" Consuelo asked, worry sneaking into her voice. She didn't touch the money. Her fingers hesitated, hovering over it.

Santiago laughed. "It's money. What? You don't know money when you see it?"

"But where did you get it? I thought they fired you from Burger King."

"No one fired me. I quit that place," Santiago said. He grabbed a Coke from the refrigerator and downed it without pausing for air.

No one said a word. Their minds were racing with speculations.

"And that's just the beginning, Mom," he continued. "I got this new job. It's going to pay me a lot of money, you'll see. You won't have to worry about anything anymore. I'm going to take care of you now." Santiago smiled, puffing out his chest. A country melody chirped from his phone. Santiago said he had to go. He helped himself to a *pan dulce* and took off, leaving the group in a stunned state of silence.

Abuelita Alpha sniffed loudly, breaking the uncomfortable stillness.

Fabi's aunt Consuelo turned on her quickly. "Don't you dare!"

"Did I say anything?" Abuelita Alpha retorted. Her eyes were growing large. "But if he's hanging out with those Salinas boys now, nothing good will come out of it, you hear me?"

Consuelo stood up. "I can't listen to this." She grabbed her purse and stormed out the door.

"The truth burns. Burns like the holy cross," Abuelita Alpha mumbled to herself as she sipped the cup of coffee in front of her. "That child is a bad seed. I always thought so."

"Mamá!" Magda cried, shocked.

"Don't tell me you weren't thinking it! *Por el árbol se conoce el fruto.*"

"Ya basta!" Leo called out. *Enough!* "Santiago is a good kid. Sure, he gets in trouble, but who didn't at his age? He didn't rob Chuy. And I don't want to hear any more gossip about this unless you have proof. We all know how gossip spreads like wildfire here."

Abuelita Alpha huffed loudly in disapproval, crossing her arms and legs, but Fabi sighed with relief. She hated to think her cousin could do such a thing, and she hated everyone talking about him behind his back like this.

Just then Fabi's phone vibrated in her back pocket. It was a text from Santiago saying to meet him behind the restaurant. Leonardo and Magda had gone into the kitchen to discuss the incident in private. Quiet murmurs started again from the table. Fabi mumbled some excuse about watering the cactus, not that any-one noticed, and slid out of the room.

The screen door slammed loudly behind her. It was a cloudy night and she didn't even have the stars to help orient her. She turned on the light switch. The dull yellow glow from the bulb over-head created shadows that jumped out from the corners, trash cans, and random junk her dad dumped back there. An owl hooted from behind the shed. It reminded her of the stories she heard as a kid of *La Lechuza*, the witch who could turn into an owl, predicting death. Of course, Fabi didn't believe in those scary bedtime tales. But the soft hooting still made her kind of nervous.

Then a figure jumped out from the shadows and grabbed her.

"Aghhhhhhh!" Fabi cried, jumping.

Santiago started to laugh and then he said in a scary old lady voice, "*La Lechuza* is coming to get you."

"*Not. Funny.*" Fabi punched his shoul-der. She didn't want to admit he really scared her, and was thinking of the exact same scary story.

Santiago laughed harder, practically dou-bled over in hysterics. "You should see your face. I thought you were going to wet your pants."

Fabiola couldn't believe him, pulling pranks after what had just happened. "What do you want, Santiago? Why did you call me out here?"

Santiago wiped his eyes and finally regained control. "It's not a big deal. I just need you to hold something for me. You got the key for the shed, right?"

A warning light flashed in Fabi's mind. "Why? Why do you want the key? Why not just ask my dad?"

"Whoa," said Santiago, putting his hands up in a "calm down" gesture. "What's up with the twenty questions?"

"Did you know that Chuy was beaten up and robbed today?"

Santiago looked stunned.

"Right in front of the restaurant. Did you know that he was covering for me tonight? He wasn't even supposed to be here," she said, all her worry and guilt coming out in a rush.

"Wait!" Santiago interrupted. "Do you think I had something to do with that?"

Fabiola hated herself for suspecting him. It felt so wrong. But she didn't know what to believe anymore. "Well, you tell me."

"Is it because I gave my mom money?" Santiago turned away. He cursed under his breath. Then he said, "I swear that I had nothing to do with what happened to Chuy."

Fabi stared at him for a minute. She really wanted to believe him, but there was a little seed of doubt in her mind.

Santiago held on to her gaze until finally, she relented. "Okay, I'm sorry," Fabi said, feeling calmer. "I don't know what I was thinking. This whole thing has me jumpy."

"It's cool." Santiago bit his lower lip, thinking. "Hey, so do you think I can store something in that shed?" He motioned at the metal storage unit.

"What is it?" Fabi pulled out her keys from her back pocket.

Santiago's eyes lit up and he ran to the alley. He came back carrying a crate of metal objects.

Fabi unlocked the shed and slid the door open. He unloaded several more crates and stacked them on top of each other. She glanced at the round metal cylinders. Hubcaps — expensive hubcaps. She pulled one out.

"So . . ."

Santiago carried the last crate into the shed. "You wouldn't believe me," he told her.

"Try me."

Santiago stopped and leaned against the shed. "Well, I was on my way to the football game when I found this box truck that was deserted on the side of the road. The rear door was rolled halfway up. I was curious, so I took a look. . . ."

"You stole them!"

"I found them, all right? I didn't steal nothing. I told you I *found* them."

"Is that how you're making all that money?"

Santiago licked his lips. "I don't like where this conversation is going. I appreciate you doing me this favor. But the less you know, the better. I just want to wait a little, you know. I promise I'm going to move it. I'm going to sell them, too, all legit, because that's the kind of guy I am," he promised.

"Okay, Santiago." Fabi didn't like any of it, but she didn't want to nag him, either. "Sometimes the things you do just seem wrong for some reason. So just . . . be careful, all right?"

Santiago smiled. "Always. I better go." He waved and said, "Later, cuz," before heading back to the alley where his truck was parked.

As Fabiola watched him drive off, she had a bad feeling about this situation, but she also knew she couldn't control her cousin. No matter how much she might want to, she couldn't save him from himself.

chapter 6

The buzz from the first football game continued to race through the halls the following week. Crowds burst into cheers whenever a football jock stepped into the halls — even if he was a benchwarmer. But Fabiola couldn't share in the school's celebratory mood. She wanted to, but she just couldn't stop thinking about the mugging. It felt so personal. It could have been her. It *should've* been her. Worse was the feeling that everyone in her family blamed Santiago. Fabi still wasn't sure what to think, and either way, Santiago wasn't making things any easier with his new hub-caps business.

Just before lunch, Fabi spotted her sister walking with a bunch of her friends to the cafeteria.

"Hey, sis, how's it going?"

Alexis just shrugged her shoulders, waving her friends to go on ahead. "Okay, I guess. I can't believe I missed the first high school football game of the season. Sounds like everyone was there."

Fabi couldn't believe her ears. "What?"

"You know what I mean." She squeezed Fabi's hand. "If Mom hadn't forgotten her wallet, we wouldn't have stopped at the restaurant. It just kinda sucks, you know — timing."

They grabbed their food and headed to an empty table. Fabi struggled with her feelings. How could her sister be so selfish? Chuy had been mugged, and by someone they probably knew. Wasn't that freaky? Shouldn't everyone be worried that there was some crazed mugger among them? And wasn't it actually *good* timing that they'd found Chuy before his injuries had gotten much worse?

Fabi shook her head to clear it. She just wanted to be normal for a second, so she tried to change the subject.

"Do you need a ride to your voice class today? I think Santiago is —"

Alexis was staring over Fabi's shoulder. A sly smile danced on her face. "I think I have a ride."

"Hey, Alexis." Dex Andrews leaned on the table, gazing at Alexis and of course completely ignoring Fabi. "Missed you at the game last Friday."

Alexis blushed, tossing her hair flirtatiously. "I know. I hate myself for missing it, but I had this family emergency."

"Everything okay?" Dex asked.

She waved her hand in a "forget it, it's nothing" gesture. "Don't worry about it."

"I know what you need," Dex said as he pulled a yellow rose from behind his back and offered it to Alexis with a great flourish.

Alexis giggled as she accepted the rose.

Dex smiled, looking relieved. "Would you like to join me for lunch?" He motioned toward the jock and cheerleader tables. Then he put his hands together in a pleading gesture that obviously made Alexis weak in the knees. Before she'd actually managed to say anything, Dex grabbed Alexis's lunch tray and started for the other side of the cafeteria.

Fabi watched in shock as her sister crossed into jock territory. Alexis couldn't care less about *the rules*. She did as she pleased — just like *she always did*.

"Hey, can I sit here?" a familiar voice asked. Fabi looked up at a blue lunch tray. Milo stood there, bobbing his head to some music on his iPod. Fabi wanted to tell him to leave her alone, but before she could, he plunked down across from her. Milo dug into his messy chili and cheese dog with gusto. But Fabi had lost her appetite and threw the baby carrot that she'd been holding back onto the tray in front of her.

Milo noted Fabi's silence. "Are you okay? That was crazy about your friend the other day. It reminded me of some of the hate crimes I saw in Phoenix. But I never saw nothing like that, you know, up close."

"Hate crime?" Fabi asked, startled. "Who would hate Chuy? He doesn't do anything but work hard. He goes to school. And he's supporting his family in Mexico."

"Where I'm from," Milo said between bites, "being brown is reason enough for getting jumped."

She flinched. "Really? That wouldn't happen here."

"No? Why not?"

"'Cause we're all Mexican," Fabi said, motioning around the room. Anyone could see she was right. The school was 80 percent Hispanic, with

just a sprinkling of whites and a few other eth-
nicities. Despite Milo's comment, she refused to
believe that Chuy was the victim of a hate crime.

Sure, she was aware of the anti-immigrant
and anti-Mexican attitudes across the country.
She saw lots of it on TV. And people were getting hurt. But that kind of stuff never happened
in the Valley.

"Hey, Fabi, I need to ask you a favor," Milo
said, interrupting her thoughts. When he
paused, Fabi nodded for him to go on. But Milo
squirmed.

"What is it?" she asked, leaning over the
table to hear him better.

Milo bit his lip nervously. "Well, it's kind of
embarrassing."

"Spit it out."

"Okay, well, I have this gig, and they gave
me money for treats and stuff, and I agreed
because I thought they just wanted chips and
salsa, but apparently treats means something
different here in South Texas. And I was thinking

since your family runs that restaurant and everything . . ."

"Yes?"

"Can you teach me about Texas barbecue? By Saturday?"

Dex started taking Alexis to her weekly vocal classes after school. It was fine with Fabiola; she didn't like the idea of her sister waiting for a ride after dark. Alexis wanted to be her own person at school. Fabi couldn't hate her for that, but she did miss hanging out. *Things change*, she told herself as she put on an apron at work.

Business was usually slow on Wednesday afternoons; only the regular local customers were in. The senior-citizen brigade was there, reading the obituaries and drinking coffee. Grandma Trini was feeding mashed beans to Baby Oops.

Fabi's mother came up to her, wearing a matching apron over her dark floral dress. "Where's your sister?"

"Voice class," Fabi answered, pinning her hair out of her face.

Magda looked at her for a second. "Her teacher just called and said that she needed to reschedule class for another day."

"Oh, that's right." Fabi thought quickly. "Alexis mentioned that to me after school and said that she was going to stay at the library for a study group."

"Study group?"

Fabi nodded and turned quickly to pick up some napkins and silverware. Now she was lying so her sister could hang out with Dex Andrews. *Perfect.*

As the day turned into evening, Alexis finally snuck into Garza's behind a group of new customers. Fabiola grabbed her sister's hand the minute she caught sight of her and pulled her into the hallway that led to the bathrooms. "You sneaky little —" It took all of Fabi's strength to hold back her words. But this was not the time or the place. "I don't know where you've been, but your vocal coach called —"

"Oh, crap," Alexis interrupted, slapping her forehead with her hand. Fabi grabbed Alexis's wrist and pulled it away from her face.

"What's that?" Fabi demanded.

Alexis blushed, but there was a hint of pride in the way she fingered the new silver chain with a sparkly letter pendant around her neck. "Oh, this, it's nothing. Dex —"

"No, those things on your *neck*?" Fabi demanded, pointing to two large, round love bites under her sister's new necklace.

Alexis's eyes grew wide with shock. "Oh, no!" she cried, covering her throat with her hands. "What am I going to do?"

"There's makeup under the sink," Fabi said, exasperated. Her sister's charades were going to drive her crazy!

Alexis ran into the bathroom. "Oh, and I told Mom that you'd gone to a study group after school," Fabi called after her.

"Fabiola!" her father's deep voice boomed from the kitchen. She stomped her foot in irritation. Why did everyone always have to call her for everything?

The restaurant picked up for the dinner rush. Between orders, Fabi noticed Alexis arguing with her mother and then storming out of the restaurant. She prayed that her mother didn't find out about her little lie. If only Alexis had told her that she wasn't going to her class, then maybe she could have covered for her better. But then again, Fabi thought, why was she even covering for her? The whole family was convinced that Alexis was going to be a singing sensation. She'd received special treatment, voice and music classes, since she was eight years old and won a singing contest at the stock and trade show. But now, she was throwing it all away for a make-out session with Dex.

At the end of her shift, Fabiola began to

count her tips. Her mother came over and sat across from her. She took off one of her two-inch heels and began to massage her swollen feet.

"What are you going to do with all that money you save?" her mother asked. "You never buy anything nice for yourself. Isn't that the shirt you got for free at the rodeo last year?"

"I don't need anything, Mom," Fabi said, sliding all the coins into her coin purse.

"You're saving to run away from us, aren't you?" Magda teased — but her eyes betrayed real worry behind her joke.

"I wish! As if you guys would ever let me," Fabi said, pretending to sound upset. She looked at the tattered coin purse. It held all her dreams. "I just want to see the world one day." Her mother stared back with a bewildered expression, and Fabi added, "Haven't you ever wanted to go to Venice? Or see the temples of Machu Picchu?"

Instead of answering, Magda began to fidget with the fake white flowers on the table. Fabi watched out of the corner of her eye, pretending to play with the clasp of the coin purse.

Finally, her mother looked down at her lap and said, "I don't know where you get these crazy ideas. They must be from your dad's side of the family." The pained look on her mother's face made Fabi feel terrible about what she'd said. She didn't have the right words to explain this urge she had to run, run far away — and what could she say that wouldn't make her mother feel like she wanted to run away from *her*?

So she changed the subject. "What's up with Alexis?"

Her mother seemed relieved. "Your sister is just in a hurry to grow up. She wants to go to some party this weekend. I told her *no*." Magda looked at Fabi to read her reaction. "I don't care. She can hate me all she wants. She's only fourteen. You know how your sister gets. She can't take no for an answer. With Chuy out, we need her help here. But for Alexis, everything is the *end of the world*."

Fabi smiled sympathetically. That was Alexis, all right.

On Saturday night, Fabiola left the restaurant early to help with Milo's party. She pulled on her favorite pair of skinny jeans and a cute sequined top she'd bought with Georgia Rae last summer, but never wore. Then she opened the makeup tote box she got on her twelfth birthday. Most of the cosmetics were still sealed in their packaging — gifts from the Mary Kay and Avon representatives in the family. As she applied some lip liner she couldn't help but feel butter-flies in her stomach. It had been so long since she went out and didn't have to be responsible for anyone. Her phone beeped, letting her know that Georgia Rae was outside and ready to go.

They arrived at the party as the sun started to set, casting warm reddish-orange streaks in the sky. Her phone beeped again — the fifth text from Milo since she'd left. He was really anxious about this grilling business!

The fancy house on the north side of the tracks was hidden behind a high wooden fence and ash trees. Fabi smelled smoke and heard a huge crash. The two girls raced straight from the truck toward the noise.

Soon they found what the commotion was all about — from the back porch, flames licked the stucco roof of the redbrick ranch home. Milo was inside a cloud of smoke, unsuccessfully trying to douse the flames with a bucket of water.

"Get away from there!" Fabi shouted, waving for Milo to move out of the way before he hurt himself. She turned off the flames on the gas burner. There was a shriveled piece of burnt meat on the grill. It disintegrated into powdered ash when she tried to pick it up.

Fabi turned to Milo and couldn't help but burst out laughing at his shocked expression. "Don't they teach you boys how to light a grill in Arizona?"

He shook his head in frustration. "I had no idea what I was getting into when I promised to cater. What was I thinking? This was a big mistake. Look what I did to the meat. I ruined everything."

Fabi hurried into the house, finding the kitchen and an apron that she tied around her waist. Back outside she smiled at Milo. "Why don't you fix up your music and leave the food to me," she told him. Then she quickly assessed the ingredients she had to work with — and decided it was a good thing she could send Georgia Rae to the store for more food.

By the time the guests arrived, Fabi was ready. She tried to watch casually while her schoolmates checked out the food she'd made. Seeing the satisfaction in their eyes as they tried her specialties — carne asada, fresh salsa, and guacamole — made her smile. Not too bad, she thought, for throwing it together at the last minute. She also made some veggie shish kebabs, which were the hit of the evening.

Milo was bumping to his beats on the turntables. His fingertips expertly mixed Mexican, pop, and rap dance rhythms like a chef stirring together different spices. Everyone seemed to be having a good time eating, dancing, and drinking. Fabi tried to stay away from the drinkers. She didn't like being out of control and especially didn't trust a lot of the guys to keep their hands to themselves. But after much cajoling from her classmates, she gave in to a wine cooler slushy that someone brought her — it was gross, but she drank some of it, trying to loosen up and have fun like everyone else. After all, Georgia Rae was driving.

They partied into the night, watching the moon rise over the ash and oak trees in the backyard. Guests streamed in and out of the house through a glass sliding door. Milo was jumping around his DJ station making faces at her. Fabi couldn't stop laughing. She felt kind of lightheaded and kept bumping into people as she danced. She had to find the bathroom.

"Oh, sorry," Fabi said, accidentally colliding with a group of girls dancing together in a circle.

"Watch it, *gorda*," Melodee spat, pushing her back.

This town is just too small. Fabi sighed and continued to make her way toward the house and the bathroom as if she hadn't heard that comment. Would she ever escape people like Melodee Stanton?

Fabi pushed through the crowd into the hallway. She hoped it led to a bathroom. There were a bunch of closed doors — some locked. At the very end she found the restroom. Upon opening it, hot air pressed at her. It was so stuffy that she had to open a window. Standing on top of the toilet, Fabi poked her head out to breathe in a breath of fresh air. But what she inhaled instead was marijuana smoke. She jerked back, coughing. Fabi was about to close the window when she heard a voice drifting up along with all the smoke.

"Bro, it was so easy. They practically give you their money. . . . Sure, I roughed them up a bit. . . . You have to, nothing really bad, just having a little fun. . . . Nah, there's nothing to worry about. They won't tell the cops. They don't want to get deported, that's the best part. They're like walking ATMs, man. Walking ATMs."

Fabi felt like she'd been smacked sober. She'd recognize Dex's bragging voice anywhere. It took all of her strength to keep from peeking back out the window. Who was he talking to? Who else was in on this? He was definitely talking about illegal immigrants. Was Dex responsible for what happened to Chuy?

Someone banged loudly on the door. Fabi jumped, afraid that she'd been caught spying. But there was nowhere to hide. The door banged again. Fabi was trapped. Slowly, she flushed the toilet and opened the door. Thankfully, it was just some girl who needed to throw up.

Back in the living room, Fabi found Georgia Rae dancing with a boy from the debate team. Fabi grabbed her hand. "We have to go."

"Now?" Georgia Rae stared back at her, bewildered. "I thought we were having fun."

Just then Dex walked through the front door with two other jocks. Fabi could feel his eyes on her. He knew! She spun around, looking for another exit. All of a sudden a girl screamed, a high-pitched drunken wail. It was Melodee and she was running to Dex, like a toddler seeing her daddy at the end of the day. Dex ducked under one of his boys and spun away, leaving Melodee to fall headfirst into the couch, where a couple was entangled in each other's arms. A few of the people nearby laughed at Melodee's expense.

"Please," Fabi pleaded, grabbing Georgia Rae's hand. "If you don't give me a ride, I'll find someone else."

"Fine," Georgia Rae huffed in annoyance, and wiped the sweat off her brow. She said good-bye to a couple of friends while Fabi went to grab their stuff from under Milo's turntables.

Fabi led Georgia Rae to the glass side doors. Her heart was racing. Dex was once again making his way toward her. Thankfully, the mass of dancing bodies was slowing him down.

Just as she was about to get out of the house, the glass door slid open in front of Fabi and Alexis stepped inside. Fabi stopped in her tracks. She glanced back and saw Dex wave at Alexis. Dex wasn't coming to get Fabi. He was coming for Alexis, who didn't even have permission to be out tonight.

"What are you doing here?" Fabi cried, despite herself.

Alexis shot her a sneaky grin. "What does it look like I'm doing? I came to party." Alexis began to nod to the music, glancing eagerly around the room.

Fabi shook her head. "Mom said you weren't allowed to be here."

"Oh, come on, Fabiola," Alexis groaned, rolling her eyes. "Why are you always trying to ruin everything? Stop acting like my mother."

"Your *mother*?" Fabi yelled. She was livid and couldn't control herself. Her hand reached out and pushed Alexis out the door, hard. Alexis cried out as Fabi followed her and started pulling her away from the house.

"Ouch! Stop it!" Alexis tried to fight her sister off, slapping wildly. But all those years carrying heavy plates had given Fabi strong, solid arms. Alexis didn't have a chance. Fabi half-pushed, half-dragged Alexis to the street.

"I hate you!" Alexis cried, beginning to sob. "You are such a bully. You never let me do anything. It's not fair! I wish you weren't my sister. I wish I didn't *have* a sister."

Fabi was speechless. She shoved Alexis into Georgia Rae's truck and jumped inside next to her, breathing heavily as her sister cried and her best friend got in and started the engine.

The tension in the car was suffocating, but Fabi couldn't break the silence. She wanted to tell them about what she'd heard, but she didn't know how to begin. And besides, she couldn't believe what a brat Alexis was being!

Georgia Rae drove in silence. The night was dark and empty.

"How did you even get out here?" Fabi finally asked.

Alexis stared angrily out the front window.

"Alexis, tell me!"

"I ran, okay?" Alexis shouted back, crossing her arms in front of her chest. "I ran."

Fabi just shook her head. Alexis would do *anything* to get what she wanted.

chapter 7

Georgia Rae pulled the truck to a stop in front of the Garzas' old white bungalow. The paint was flaking off the planks of wood like old skin. Leonardo had promised to repaint it, but he never had the time. As soon as the truck had stopped completely, Alexis climbed over her sister and jumped out, slamming the passenger door in Fabi's face.

"Alexis, we have to talk!" Fabi cried, yanking the truck door back open and following her sister up the front walk.

"I'm not talking to you!" Alexis slammed the

metal gate to their yard, making a loud clang. Inside the house, their baby brother started to cry. Then a light blazed on behind the curtains. Fabiola squeezed her eyes shut in frustration.

"Can you at least try to keep it down?" Fabi hissed. "People are trying to sleep."

"Be quiet. Go to class. Talk to these people. Don't talk to those," Alexis spat in a mocking voice. "I'm tired of you always bossing me around, telling me who I can and can't be friends with. You're such a hypocrite. You think you're better than everyone, but then you go and party with those same people and tell me I can't!"

"Alexis —"

The porch light came on, illuminating the sisters standing toe-to-toe.

"No, Fabi. You can't tell me what to do anymore. I'm not a little girl."

"I know that."

"Do you? Do you really? Look at me." Alexis stood taller in her too-tight shirt and painted-on jeans. "I'm practically grown. I can make my own decisions." She locked eyes with her sister. "I'm not like you. I'm sorry high school sucks for you. I really am. But I don't want to be you. I want to be my own person. Why can't you just understand that?"

Her words stung like a hard slap across the face. Fabiola wanted to shrink into a little ball and cry, but just then the front door opened. Their dad, wearing a faded Spurs T-shirt and boxer shorts, filled the doorway with a menacing frown. Behind him, their baby brother wailed as Magda tried to rock him back to sleep.

"What is the meaning of this?" Leonardo demanded.

"I don't want to talk about it!" Alexis said as she pushed her way past her father. "I hate you. I hate all of you!" she cried, storming down the hall and slamming her bedroom door.

Leonardo turned to Fabi for an explanation. He folded his arms in front of his chest.

Fabi cowered under his disapproving stare. She couldn't stand to disappoint her family.

"It's not what you think —"

"So, what is it?"

Fabi paused and licked her lips. Her throat felt really dry. "I'm the one who dragged her home."

"What was your sister doing out? You know she is not allowed to go out."

"I don't know. I was just as shocked to see her show up at the party."

"Fabiola." Her father sighed. She could feel the disappointment in his voice. "You are responsible for your sister. You know that. Your mom and I can't do everything. It's hard enough running the restaurant, especially with your new baby brother. . . . There are a lot of people depending on us."

"I understand."

"I don't think you do." Leonardo sniffed. "Have you been drinking?"

"No, I swear. Okay, so maybe a little sip."

His eyes blazed with anger. "Don't lie to me!"

"I'm trying not to!"

"Just stop! Stop talking. I can't trust you just to watch your little sister. You can forget about the trip to New York with your aunt."

"But, Dad, that's my quince —" Fabi reached out to him, but he jerked away. She tried again. "You don't understand. I had nothing to do with what Alexis —"

Leonardo raised his calloused hand in a threatening manner and Fabi jumped back instinctively. Her dad caught himself and stopped. He would never hit her, but the moment startled them both.

After a moment Leonardo glanced at his watch and cursed. "Get changed."

At first Fabi thought he meant she should put on her pajamas, but then he added, "Put on some old jeans and a T-shirt. We're leaving."

"But, Dad, it's almost two thirty in the morning."

"That's right," he snapped, shuffling toward the bathroom. "If I can't go back to bed, neither can you. You're going to help me scrub down the restaurant. Top to bottom!"

By eight the next morning, Fabiola was ready to pass out on top of the counter. Her whole body ached from scrubbing the floor on her hands and knees all morning. Garza's was due for an inspection from the Texas Department of Health. A couple of years ago, they were fined severely, almost losing the restaurant, because they used her uncle's goat meat, which wasn't USDA certified. So now her dad wasn't going to risk a single infraction.

In addition, Santiago kept bugging her about his merchandise. He showed up as the restaurant opened and Fabi couldn't deal with his incessant pestering, so finally she handed him her keys. She popped a handful of gumdrops into her mouth and washed them back with some Coke, hoping all the sugar would help keep her awake a little longer.

"Child, you are practically going to fall

asleep standing up," Grandma Trini scolded. "Take a break. Sit."

Fabiola joined her grandmother's table. She greeted the other people there: Officer Bobby Sanchez, a distant cousin with pockmarked skin; Cynthia Perales, a school librarian; and City Councilman Rey Garcia III, who moonlighted as an insurance salesman. Trini was filling them in on the details of the mugging. Almost a week later it was still on everyone's mind.

The councilman bit off the tip of a corn tortilla that he had rolled in his right hand. "I've been telling Leonardo to put up security cameras for years now."

"But stuff like that never happened before," Cynthia pointed out, wiping the side of her mouth with a paper napkin. "Dos Rios is changing. There are a lot of new faces now. Families are coming over in droves. We can hardly keep up with all the new students."

"Well, I hear that's how it starts," Trini whispered, leaning in. Fabi was embarrassed by her grandmother's super-low-cut shirt and hoped Trini wouldn't spill out — again. "The *cárteles* mug the poor *mojaditos* and force them to do their bidding. That's how they get tangled in the gangster life."

Officer Sanchez, who'd been quiet for most of the conversation, cleared his throat. He was a man of few words, but when he spoke, everyone listened. "It's not the *cárteles*." He flicked crumbs off his uniform dismissively. "Too small-time. Sounds like some *huercos* just fooling around."

"Dex Andrews did it," Fabi blurted out. Everyone turned to her. Their surprised expressions switched to disbelief, and then they all started to crack up. Loudly. Her grandmother Trini laughed the loudest, slamming her hand on the table.

"Fabiola," her grandmother cried between chuckles as she tried to regain control of herself. "Your sister told me you were jealous, but this is too much."

Fabiola could feel her face getting hot.

"I'm not jealous," she stammered, feeling ridiculous.

"Fabi." The school librarian looked at her over the top of her glasses. "If you can't say anything nice, don't say anything at all."

"That's a serious accusation you just made," Officer Sanchez said, cleaning off his plate with a piece of tortilla. "I wouldn't say that kind of stuff without proof."

Councilman Garcia gestured for Officer Sanchez to relax. "Hey, Bobby, don't you remember being a teen? I know it's been a while, but try. I'm sure Fabiola was just kidding. It's hard to be the oldest. I'm the oldest of ten. You have all the responsibility without any of the fun," he said, winking to her in understanding. "I'm sure she didn't mean to accuse Dex Andrews of anything. Right, Fabiola?"

Fabiola wanted to kick him — kick all three of them. Dex Andrews, for all purposes, was untouchable. He was a football star and his family owned the town's Amway business, where locals purchased their animal feed and house products. Even more important, his grand-father was a judge.

"Did you see the catch he made in the fourth quarter?" the councilman gloated. "Andrews has the fastest feet in the entire Valley, I tell you. He just appeared at the five-yard line like nothing. You heard it from me, that boy is going places." The conversation switched to high school foot-ball and then turned to Valley politics. Fabiola had enough and snuck away without notice.

On Monday, Fabiola tried to talk to her sister at school, with no success. She wanted to warn her about Dex, about what she'd overheard at the party. But Alexis was having nothing to do with her. She was grounded for a month and she blamed Fabi — as if Fabi forced her to sneak out and disobey their parents. So now, Alexis was making a point of ignoring her in the hallways, using Dex and her new friends as a shield. But two could play at that game, Fabi thought, heading to the library at lunch. A part of her was relieved not to have to cover for her sister anymore.

Still, Fabiola couldn't help but wonder if her sister had a point. Was she overreacting? Maybe she misheard Dex? She did catch only part of the conversation. And maybe she *was* jealous? Alexis didn't need help making friends and being popular. She was doing a good job of that all by herself. Maybe it was *Fabi* who needed help making friends. Fabiola watched her sister across the lunchroom. Alexis was changing — and she wasn't just talking about the new hairstyle and heavy makeup. The world as Fabi knew it was shifting around her and there was nothing she could do to stop it.

Several days later, a phone call in the middle of the night woke Fabi from her unsettling dreams. It was Chuy. He was panting heavily and talking fast — so fast he didn't even try to speak English. It took her a minute to figure out what he was saying. He begged her to come to the restaurant, right away, and not to tell her parents. Fabi pulled on a pair of jeans and a shirt from the floor and snuck out her bedroom window.

She ran down the street, her flip-flops slapping loudly on the concrete sidewalk. The street was empty this time of night. The dull yellow glow from the streetlamp created even more shadows than she remembered. Shadows where muggers and rapists could lurk. She hurried her feet and listened closely for any noise that could be threatening. The lights of the restaurant burned bright on the lonely street. It filled Fabi with relief.

Finally, she pushed open the door and was greeted by the comforting chime. But what she saw inside was beyond disturbing. It made her want to scream.

Tables were turned over. Chairs were thrown on their sides. Her mother's careful plastic floral arrangements were tossed all over the floor. Was it a robbery? There was a man on the floor and others standing over him. Fabi reached out for the first thing she could grab for protection.

"Fabiola," a voice called out. She screamed, swinging the broom wildly. Chuy came up behind her and took the broom from her hands. He looked like he'd just been in a scuffle. His hair was disheveled and there was a big tear in his shirt.

Catching her breath, Fabi glanced around. "What happened here?" The guy was still on the floor, and now she could see he was tied up with red tablecloths and gagged with a cloth napkin. Over him stood a couple of guys she'd seen hanging around with Chuy sometimes. His friends, she thought.

Chuy was jumping around nervously. "I knew he'd be back," he said in hurried Spanish. "I knew it was just a matter of time. I knew your parents wouldn't believe me. I had to catch him, okay? Catch him in the act."

"Catch who? Catch the guy who beat you up?"

Chuy nodded. Then he gestured at the tied-up prisoner. The guy looked somewhat familiar under a black eye. Her heart fluttered with recognition. But, no! It couldn't be. She rushed over to the prisoner struggling at his binds.

It was Santiago.

"Santiago, oh, my God! What's going on?" She removed his gag.

A string of curses came out of her cousin's mouth. He thrashed and floundered like a fish out of water, trying to free himself.

"I knew no one would believe me," Chuy explained, over Fabiola's shoulder, in Spanish. "That's why I asked my friends to keep an eye on the place."

Her cousin was beaten up bad. Tears welled up in Fabi's eyes. She couldn't believe it was Santiago.

"Fabi," Santiago called to her. "Don't believe this punk. He's lying. I didn't do nothing."

"Mentiroso!" Chuy shouted back.

"Fabi, Fabi, you have to believe me. I didn't

[127]

do it," Santiago pleaded. "I just came to get my stuff. You remember the stuff you helped me hide. And then I got hungry, so since I had your keys —"

Suddenly, the door chimed again behind them. A cool breeze blew in. Fabi's breath caught. Her father, mother, and Alexis with their baby brother in her arms stood at the entrance. The baby started to cry, sensing the shock and anxiety in the air. Behind them, Fabi saw the familiar red and blue blinking lights of a police car.

chapter 8

Fabi flinched as she heard the sharp click of the handcuffs locking around Santiago's wrists. She turned away, still unwilling to believe it. "You can't let them do this, Dad. Dad?"

Her family stared from the sidelines as Officer Sanchez bowed Santiago's head down and into the cop car. It was so surreal. Fabi wondered if she was dreaming. She turned to her mother. Magda's face was ghost white.

"I have to call Consuelo," her mother mumbled in a daze. She was still in her night robe and slippers.

"What happened, Fabi?" Alexis asked, hugging the baby tightly to her chest. She'd forgotten, in all the panic, that she wasn't speaking to her sister.

"I don't really know. Chuy called me and told me to come over. I guess they were trying to catch whoever jumped him and they caught Santiago."

Chuy motioned for them to sit at a table. He brought coffee.

Leonardo plopped into a chair. He rubbed his thick fingers through his close-cropped hair in frustration. "I don't understand. What was Santiago doing here in the middle of the night? What were you guys doing here?" He gestured at Chuy and his friends. "How did he get in?"

Fabi squirmed. Her father noticed and turned to her, waiting for a response. She thought about lying, but Santiago was already in enough trouble.

"I gave him my keys."

"You did what?" her father shouted, jumping out of his seat, while his chair flew back, crashing onto the floor.

"Dad, it's Santiago. *Our* Santiago. He was storing some stuff in the storage unit out back and he was just coming by to pick it up."

Chuy cut in. "I know nothing about a storage room. I saw beams from a flashlight and heard laughing and the sound of something breaking."

Leonardo slammed his fist down on the table, making all the cups of coffee jump. "That boy has gone too far! I defended him at first. Poor kid has had a hard life, but this, *this*, is too much. My nephew needs to learn that there are consequences for his actions."

"What are you saying?" Fabi asked, alarmed. Looking around the table, she could tell that everyone thought Santiago was guilty of attacking Chuy. "It doesn't make sense. If Santiago wanted to mug someone, why would he come into the restaurant when no one was around?" She turned to Chuy. He stared back at her, confused. "You were mugged in front of the store, not inside, right?"

Her dad crossed his arms. "What are you trying to get at?"

"Well, we're talking about muggings, not robberies."

"Is there a difference?"

"I know Santiago looks really guilty right now. And I'm sure the hubcaps back there are stolen." She motioned toward the storage area.

"Hubcaps," her father repeated in a low growl.

"Santiago may be a lot of things. But I can't believe that he would beat you up, Chuy." Fabi reached a hand out to Chuy, but he jerked away from her.

The cook stared at her with a cold expression and said in Spanish, "I knew your parents wouldn't believe me unless Santiago was caught and they saw it with their own eyes. But you,

Fabiola, I thought you were different." Chuy got up and cleared the table.

"Chuy," Fabi called out, but he refused to look at her. He gathered his stuff and went home.

Fabi had to wait until nine in the morning to visit Santiago. The police had thrown the book at him. They were accusing him of breaking and entering, destroying private property, and receiving stolen property. They had also thrown in, for good measure, assault and battery on several undocumented migrant workers who had ended up in the hospital with severe beatings, based on Chuy's testimony.

Everyone was so quick to blame Santiago, Fabi thought as Delia Zavala, the police secretary, let her into a small, windowless room. Grandma Trini and Abuelita Alpha had come along, too, each dressed for the occasion — in black.

When they brought Santiago in, he was quite a sight: His face was all black and blue, and one eye was swollen shut. He had bloody scratch marks on his forehead and cheek. It was horrible, and made Fabi sick to her stomach.

"Oh, my baby," Grandma Trini cried, rushing over to him. He winced at her touch. "Have you seen a doctor? Delia," she cried over her shoulder, "you better call the doctor quick. If my baby gets an infection, I'm holding the police department responsible." She pulled out something to wipe his face, spitting onto it first. Santiago flinched when he saw that she was holding a maxi pad.

"You are not putting that on my face," he cried.

Trini sighed in annoyance. "Ay, it's not mine."

Abuelita Alpha grabbed his hand, inspecting it for marks. "Did you sell your soul?" she asked sternly.

"What?" Santiago squirmed under her gaze.

"Don't you lie to me! Did you sell your soul in blood to the Dark Prince? I need to know for the spiritual cleansing I'm going to perform. You need a *limpia.*"

Santiago mustered a giggle.

"This is no joke," Abuelita Alpha hissed heatedly. The two old women glanced at each other in silent communication. Then Abuelita Alpha nodded and opened her bag. She took out a bottle of holy water and a bouquet of rosemary stems Fabi knew she'd collected from the massive bush in front of her house that morning. *"En el nombre del Padre . . ."* she prayed loudly, throwing holy water in his face with one hand and sweeping the evil spirits off with the rosemary in the other. Santiago was really cracking up now. Abuelita Alpha smacked him hard on the head with the branches. She cursed under her breath about what a good-for-nothing, troublesome, stupid child he was.

Fabiola waited until Alpha finished her exorcism. When her grandmother fell back into the chair, Trini hurried to get her some water. Santiago was smiling, enjoying the attention.

"Santiago, do you understand how much trouble you're in?" Fabi asked, annoyed by his attitude.

"Trouble?" He looked confused. "Chuy's claims are totally bogus. I wish I *had* mugged the fool. Punk caught me off guard." He made punching gestures in the air to show them he could not be fooled twice. "Whatever," he said with a shrug. "I'll be out by lunch."

"Santiago," Fabi said sternly. She grabbed the table for effect. "They want to try you for several muggings that happened around town."

"Huh?"

"And Delia Zavala" — Fabi motioned at the secretary — "heard that they want to try you as an adult."

"What?" Santiago grew quiet. The severity of the situation finally dawned on him. "Where's your dad? He doesn't believe that I . . ."

"Santiago." Fabi struggled to keep her voice calm. She didn't want him to know how worried she actually was. "I'm going to find a way to clear your name."

"Wrap it up," Officer Sanchez's booming voice called out behind her. The man was leaning casually against the wall. He was so silent she hadn't even noticed him enter the room.

Grandma Trini shoved Fabi aside with her big hips and mumbled to Santiago, "Baby," between tight lips. "I have bolt cutters in my hair." She squinted her left eye and tilted her head in quick jerking movements up toward her dark mass of teased-up curls. "Alpha will distract Officer Sanchez and we —"

"Grandma," Fabi scolded in a hushed manner.

"It worked for my third husband, Timoteo. You remember him, Alpha, don't you?"

Officer Sanchez appeared behind them. "All right, I'm going to have to ask you ladies to leave now," he said, motioning them toward the door.

Fabi stood her ground. "But, Officer Sanchez, this is a mistake. Santiago is being falsely accused. You have to stop this. He didn't do it."

"That's not up to me to decide."

"But I told you the other day who did it!" Fabi said emphatically. "I heard him admit it at a party. No, he was bragging, *bragging* to a bunch of people about it. It's Dex Andrews and his thugs, I'm telling you! Go ask him where he was when the attacks happened. I'm sure he doesn't even have an alibi. Just go ask Dex. *Please.*"

Officer Sanchez stared blankly at Fabi. She couldn't tell if he was asleep or listening to her behind those dark aviator sunglasses.

"Who's his judge?" Grandma Alpha asked.

Officer Sanchez smirked. "I think it's Judge Andrews — Judge Dexter Andrews II."

Good gossip always traveled like wildfire in the Valley. By the following school day, everyone had heard about Santiago's assault charges and knew Fabi had accused Dex Andrews of the crime. Students she'd known since elementary school avoided her as if she was contagious. Others rudely pushed right into her, mumbling "liar" and "fat cow" under their breath. Fabi took her hurt and stuffed it deep down. She *would not* let them see her cry!

"Hey, Fatty," a male voice called out from down the hallway.

Fabi bowed her head and walked faster, desperate to escape her tormentor.

"Fatty, yo, I'm talking to you," Dex sneered, easily catching up. He grabbed her arm tightly. Fabi gulped as he spun her around like a rag doll and pinned her against the locker doors. The chattering noise of the hallways hummed into the background. Fabi could only hear the thumping of her heart beating wildly, pounding in her head.

"Stop, please," Fabi murmured, unable to hold back the tears that had started to flow freely. Dex's sneer grew bigger. There was nowhere for Fabi to run, nothing she could do.

"Hey, what're you doing?" Milo called out from somewhere behind Dex. But Fabi could only hear scuffling sounds as if Milo was struggling with Dex's football friends.

Dex turned away. He smiled approvingly at Milo — and his friends holding Milo back — then he slowly leaned into the locker, right next to Fabi's face. He was so close their noses touched.

"You got a big fat mouth, you know that?" he whispered, low enough for only her to hear. "You better be careful. Don't want to end up like your dishwasher friend." He smirked, pulling away so she could see the satisfaction in his eyes.

"Fabi? Dex! Get off her, you jerk!"

This time it was Alexis. Fabi heard a hard, demanding note in her little sister's voice.

"What's going on here?" Vice Principal Castillo asked, coming up behind them.

Dex started to laugh, pushing away from the lockers and holding his hands up innocently.

"Oh, nothing, sir. I'm just having a little chat with my girl. Isn't that right, Fabi?"

Mr. Castillo waited for a response.

Fabi studied Dex a moment. She wanted to tell on him, but her mouth was numbed with fear.

Mr. Castillo frowned and glanced at the crowd of students standing around him. "Put those cell phones away," he cried. "This is not a show! Go to class, everyone. Go now!"

Fabi heard the sound of students shuffling away from her. But she couldn't look up. The humiliation weighed down on her like a heavy stone. Why hadn't she said anything?!

"C'mon," she heard Alexis say to Dex, leading him away. The other football guys shoved Milo to the side as they followed.

Milo stood for a moment next to her, silent. He tried to put his hand on Fabi's shoulder, but his touch made her jump. "Oh, sorry. I just wanted to see if you were okay."

"She's all right," Mr. Castillo said. "She's a tough girl."

Finally, Fabi looked up — then wished she hadn't. Every face in the hallway was staring back at her. The tension in the air was maddening. It was like one of those crazy dreams where you find yourself naked — but this was no dream. People she'd considered friends were now looking away, or worse, snapping shots to put on the Internet. Melodee Stanton stood a few feet away from her, ready to pounce at the slightest provocation. Fabi bit down hard on her lower lip and ran down the hall. She couldn't face any of them, ever again.

chapter 9

Fabiola didn't go to school the following day. She told her parents she wasn't feeling well and couldn't get out of bed. With all that was going on with Santiago, Magda and Leonardo decided to just leave her alone. When Dex Andrews pulled up to her house to pick up Alexis, dread twisted in Fabi's stomach. She couldn't believe that her sister chose him over her — even after what he did at school! Santiago was probably going to jail. And Dex was going to get away with beating up immigrants because he could. The situation was so unfair. She wanted to claw at it, tear it to shreds.

Around lunchtime, Milo and Georgia Rae surprised her with an unexpected visit. They brought pizza and a bucket of mint chocolate chip ice cream.

"Guys." Fabi tried to sound annoyed, but she was really grateful to see them. "What are you doing?"

"Milo told me what happened yesterday," Georgia Rae said, giving her a sympathetic hug as she walked in. "Bastards."

"And when you didn't show up today, I called Georgia Rae and we decided to check in on you," Milo added, hands stuffed in his pockets. He scuffed the living room floor softly with his tennis shoes.

Fabiola's heart swelled and tears wet her eyes. "Thanks," she said, giving them each a hug. "You guys are the best! Come on, sit down. Let's eat this pizza." They flopped down onto the fluffy couch and dug into the meal.

They munched silently until Fabi said, "I was thinking of transferring schools. Do you think it's too late?" She picked the mushrooms off her slice for Georgia Rae.

Milo snuck a mushroom from the pile next to Georgia Rae's plate. She tried to slap his hand, but he was too quick and plopped it into his mouth. "You can't transfer," Milo said. "Not now."

"What do you mean? Of course I can transfer. Dex won. Santiago is going to jail. My sister hates me. No one at school wants to be near me. Why would I stay?"

"Yeah," Georgia Rae agreed excitedly. "You can come to McAllen High with me! We can share a room. I'm sure my mom will say yes, if I explain what happened." Her eyes were bright and she bounced a little on the couch. "It will be so cool. We'll have so much fun. Forget this town, Fabi."

Fabiola imagined herself living in McAllen with Georgia Rae. They were practically sisters already.

But then she thought about her parents. Who would make sure her dad didn't skip lunch? Who would be there to help her mother with the tables? The waitstaff was always so unreliable. And who would keep the peace between her grandmothers? And make sure Grandpa Frank got his coffee just below tepid?

"You sure Dex said that stuff about beating up, you know, immigrants?" Milo asked, playing with his crust.

"Yes!" Fabi said firmly. "I was right on the other side of the window. I heard him say that they were easy targets. That they wouldn't resist or complain to the cops because they were undocumented. That sounds just like what happened to Chuy."

Milo bit the top of his crust, thinking. "So why don't we try to catch him in the act? Get some evidence."

"You mean, like, go undercover?" Fabi asked curiously. Milo nodded. She looked at Georgia Rae.

Georgia Rae shrugged. "It would be nice to see Dex get what he deserves."

"But don't you think Dex will be lying low now? He knows that I think he did it. My big mouth blabbed it to the whole town." Fabi wanted to hit herself for not thinking of this sooner.

"Dex does have a huge ego," Georgia Rae said, holding out her hands for emphasis. "And you know how he gets when he drinks . . ."

"Maybe Chuy can help us set a trap," Fabi mused, thoughtfully tapping her finger on her lips. "I'm sure Chuy will want to get at the real culprit. What we need is someone Dex trusts. Someone he can confide in." Fabi and Georgia Rae locked eyes. Was this a stupid idea? Dex didn't trust any of them. Fabi could only think of one thing to do. "I have an idea."

"No! You're crazy. I'm not going to do it. Get out of my way," Alexis cried.

But Fabiola wouldn't budge. Alexis grabbed her by the shoulder and tried to pull her away from the door. She tugged with all her might, but couldn't move her older sister. "Get out of my room! I'm going to tell Mom."

"Go ahead," Fabi said, crossing her arms in front of her chest. "Tell her all you want. Then we can have a nice chat about how you've been ditching your vocal lessons to hang out with Dex after school. I'm sure Mom and Dad would love to hear all about your extracurricular activities."

Alexis jumped as if she'd been stung. Fabi regretted her words. They were said out of anger, but they were also true. She didn't want to blackmail her sister into helping. But Fabi was desperate. Time was running out for Santiago.

Alexis balled her hands into fists, pure hatred shining in her eyes. She jumped on Fabi, clawing at her like a wildcat. When Fabi still refused to move, tears flowed from Alexis's eyes like a dam being released.

"What is wrong with you? Why do you hate me so much?"

Fabiola was taken aback. "What's wrong with *me*? What is wrong with *you*? You're the one who's always running off with Dex and your new friends ever since you started high school. You've become this totally different person. You don't care about Chuy, you don't care about Santi —"

"Will you just stop acting so jealous? I like who I am. I like my new friends and I like Dex. Why can't you just accept me the way I am?"

"I do accept you," Fabi insisted. "I accept that you are your own person."

"Then why are you so mean to me? You said all those horrible lies about Dex. You don't even know him."

"Lies? You think I made up that stuff about Dex to hurt *you*? Oh, c'mon, Alexis. Are you for real?"

Alexis stared back blankly. "Well, didn't you? I know you don't like him," she said.

Fabi burst out laughing.

"Hey, that wasn't a joke," Alexis said. "I'm really mad at you. Stop laughing. I mean it. I'm going to tell Mom."

"I'm sorry, Alexis," Fabi said, wiping the tears from her eyes. "You've got to believe me when I tell you, I did not make up those things about Dex to make you look bad. I don't hate you. I could never hate you," she said softly, wanting to take her sister in her arms and hug her. But she didn't dare.

Alexis sniffed loudly. She looked like a raccoon with her mascara smudged everywhere. Fabi wondered about what other kinds of issues her sister might be facing. It seemed like years since they'd talked. She noticed that her sister's cell phone was thrown across the room. "Well, I don't know why you don't like Dex! Or my friends! What did they ever do to you? They're not bad people. If you weren't so crazy judgmental, you'd know that. If you just took the time to get to know them, maybe they could be your friends, too."

Fabiola felt her cheeks redden. She didn't know what to say. Alexis wiped her nose on the back of her hand. It reminded Fabi of when Alexis was small and the kids would pick on her because she always wore big, puffy dresses to play in. She was no longer that little girl who needed protection. "I'm sorry," Fabiola finally said. "I'm sorry for being . . ."

"Judgmental?"

"If I hurt you."

Alexis flopped onto her small twin bed and sighed. "I guess that's the best I'm going to get, huh?"

Fabi looked down at her shoes. Then she followed her sister's gaze to the cell on the floor. "Is everything all right?"

Alexis shrugged. "I guess, if you call getting nonstop text messages all day and night from some crazy girl who threatens to cut you if you don't stay away from her boyfriend *all right*."

"Melodee?"

Alexis nodded, then stared out the window. "So you really think Dex is responsible?"

Fabi nodded and held her breath.

"I'm really sorry about the other day at school. I thought —" Alexis paused and started again. "When Dex grabbed you like that, I got really scared. *That's* not the Dex I know. He was like a whole different person . . . and it made me wonder . . ."

"If I am wrong about this," Fabi said desperately, "I promise to never speak badly about Dex again."

Alexis crossed her legs and arms, thinking. Fabi pressed her lips together really tightly, not wanting to disturb her sister's concentration.

"Fine," Alexis huffed loudly. Fabiola breathed out the air she hadn't realized she'd been holding. "But!" Alexis added as an afterthought. "If Dex is innocent," she warned, wagging her finger in Fabi's face, "I want a public apology and your tips for the rest of the year."

The plan was brilliant in its simplicity. All Fabi needed was a confession. If Dex confessed, then Santiago would be free. And if Dex got what he deserved, everything would go back to normal, Fabi assured herself.

Alexis was the only one who wasn't convinced.

They all gathered at Fabi's house the following Friday to set the trap.

"How do you know your plan is going to work?" Alexis asked Fabi.

Fabiola looked up from helping Chuy and said, "I don't."

Alexis frowned. "Great."

Fabi continued to fidget with Chuy's hoodie. She didn't want Dex to recognize him.

"Don't you think the hoodie with the big Mexican flag is a bit much?" Alexis commented. "It's like eighty degrees outside. Why don't we just give him a big mustache and sombrero?"

"Hey," Fabi snapped. "I'm the mastermind here, not you." Then she turned to Georgia Rae and murmured, "Do you think it's too much?" Her friend shook her head. "Okay!" Fabi clapped her hands for attention. "Let's go over it again from the top."

Alexis looked around the group nervously. She was clearly starting to regret this deal, but was now in far too deep to back out. "I'm going to call Dex and invite him to get *raspas.*" *Raspas* were Fabiola's favorite treat. It was a cup of shaved ice with flavoring, whipped cream, chopped nuts, and a cherry on top.

"Don't worry, we'll be watching you from my truck," Georgia Rae cut in excitedly. Alexis still looked plenty worried.

Chuy cleared his throat. "Then I walk . . . near. I have . . . money . . . and count," he added. Fabiola was so proud he agreed to be a part of this. Although he was responsible for Santiago being in jail, he didn't want the wrong person to pay for it.

"But," Alexis interrupted, "before you walk by I need to steer the conversation to wanting to do something crazy. So don't come real fast, Chuy. Give me some time."

"Make sure you order the piña colada *raspa*," Georgia Rae reminded Alexis as she dabbed green and brown face paint around her eyes. "I hear the lady with the short hair adds real booze for extra flavor." She'd brought a big duffel bag filled with hunting apparel with her for surveillance — and scent-controlled camouflage jackets, face masks, night-vision binoculars, and gloves, just in case.

Alexis pulled the earphones from her ears and asked, "Are you even sure these things are going to work?"

Milo grabbed her earphones. "Of course they'll work. See the little mic right here?" he said as he pointed. "Just make sure the volume is all the way up and you're standing about a foot away from him. Here, look." He showed her how to record on his cell phone.

A trickle of sweat ran down the side of Alexis's face. She looked like she wanted to throw up.

"You'll be fine." Fabi put her hand on her little sister's shoulder in a reassuring way. "We'll be right there. We won't let him touch you, okay? All you need is a confession. The minute you hear it, I want you to blow the whistle and run." Alexis still looked uneasy, so Fabi added, "We'll be right there in the truck. Everything is going to be fine."

She just hoped she was right.

chapter 10

The evening was windy, throwing dirt and lit-
ter into whirling little dust devils all along the
streets of downtown Dos Rios. Fabi's stomach
rumbled, but it wasn't from lack of food. Everything was going according to plan so far, she
thought, watching customers drive up to the
shaved-ice stand. Milo, Georgia Rae, Chuy, and
she were ducking down in Georgia Rae's truck,
trying to be incognito.

"What do you see?" Milo asked, tugging on
Fabi's jacket. They only had one pair of binoculars and she was holding them. "I wish we had

some way to hear what was going on." He bit his lower lip. "I don't know about this plan of yours."

"My plan is fine. Look, I see the two of them talking. Alexis is nervous. She keeps looking around." Fabi motioned for Chuy to go. Silently, he got out of the car and crossed the street toward Alexis and Dex.

"Damn it," Georgia Rae complained. "She's totally going to ruin it."

"Give her a break," Fabi said, spying again. "Oh, look — no, I mean don't look. Stay down. Chuy is walking by. He's counting his money right in front of Dex. This is going to be perfect."

"If this works," Milo said, "I'll shave my head."

"If this works, I'll shave *my* head!" Fabi giggled.

They both turned to Georgia Rae expectantly. "Okay, fine," Georgia Rae gave in. "I'll shave my head, too."

Milo, Georgia Rae, and Fabi laughed at the thought.

"I wonder if we'll get a reward," Georgia Rae said, her voice filled with delighted anticipation of her face in the local paper. "Maybe we'll even get on TV. Wouldn't that be cool? I can see it now: 'Local Teens Catch Town Thug!' We'll be heroes."

"Bald heroes!" Milo cried, and began to laugh hysterically.

Fabi's heart swelled. The fame would be nice, but all she really cared about was proving Santiago's innocence. She raised the binoculars back to her eyes and looked for Alexis. But Alexis and Dex were gone. A nauseous feeling took her. "Guys."

"Yeah," Georgia Rae said dreamily, obviously still soaking in the hero fantasy.

"They're gone!"

"What?" shouted Milo and Georgia Rae together.

"No, wait! I see Chuy's hoodie. There are two guys with him. They look like jocks. I don't see Alexis. What the — I look away for two seconds —" Fabi jumped out of the truck without bothering to complete her sentence.

"Fabi!" Georgia Rae called after her.

Fabiola didn't look back. Her heart leapt into her throat in fright. Where was her sister? Fabi ran through the parking lot. She weaved between cars that honked as she passed. People laughed and pointed as she sprinted in her reflective hunting attire, complete with the glowing face paint Georgia Rae had insisted on applying to her cheeks. But she didn't stop until she'd reached the edge of the corner, where she finally paused and looked both ways. There was no sign of any of them. The noise from the cars cruising on the busy boulevard blocked everything else out.

Oh, no.

Fabi heard a muffled cry. She spun back. It sounded like Chuy. Where was Alexis? She ran so hard she thought she might faint. Down the street was the town cemetery. In the daylight hours the place was decorated in bright, bushy floral displays like a parade float with streamers and balloons. But at night, it seemed like the spirits of those long-deceased loved ones came out to play. Fabiola didn't believe in ghosts, but that didn't mean she liked the idea of entering the cemetery at night. In the dimming light, she made out the shape of figures near a mausoleum in the older part of the burial ground.

"Hey," Milo huffed, out of breath, coming up behind her. Georgia Rae was right behind him, carrying her hefty duffel bag. Fabi smiled, grateful for her crazy friends. She motioned for them to keep quiet while she pointed out the figures.

"What's in the bag?" Fabi whispered.

Georgia Rae dropped the bag on the dirt and unzipped it carefully, trying not to make any noise. She passed each of them headlamps to put on. Then she pulled out rope, some emergency flares, and a can of pepper spray.

"You better watch where you spray that." Fabi pointed to the can.

Georgia Rae made a "don't worry" gesture with her hand. "I've used this stuff tons of times on myself. It really doesn't hurt too much after a while."

Fabi rolled her eyes and quickly prayed that no one got hurt on this crazy mission. The three of them crouched down and snuck into the cemetery, passing marble benches and brick markers. The dried grass crunched softly under their sneakers. Sunken tombstones and angel statues created a maze to circle through. Fabi noticed the date on one of the graves. It read 1833 — when the land was still part of Mexico. Fabi and Alexis had an ancestor buried here, a great-great-great-grandfather on her mother's side who came from Spain seeking fame and fortune. Now, Fabi prayed to her nameless relative to protect her and her friends from any evil spirits and mean football players lurking in the dark.

A dull beam of light flickered off to their right. Georgia Rae, the experienced huntress, took the lead, stealthily heading toward it. Fabi had no plan. She just knew they had to rescue her sister and Chuy.

As they edged closer, Fabi could make out voices talking. Georgia Rae motioned for them to split up and surround the group. Fabi swallowed her growing anxiety and crept silently forward. Milo followed behind her. She stopped behind a large tombstone. She couldn't see anything, but she could hear their voices loud and clear.

"You know," Dex said, "I've always found cemeteries kind of sexy."

"What do you mean?" Alexis asked.

Fabi sighed in relief. Alexis was not hurt. But where was Chuy?

"There's the full moon, and you and me, here alone."

"Yeah, this is pretty cool," Alexis agreed. There was a hint of worry in her voice. "But like I said, I want to do something, you know, crazy and wild tonight."

"Well, we can be as wild as you want."

"What's the wildest thing you've ever done, Dex?"

"How 'bout I show you?"

"No, tell me."

"It's more fun if I show you."

"Dex, just tell me, all right?"

"What's your problem?" Dex asked, growing cautious. "And why do you still have those earphones on? Yo, what's this? What are you —" Suddenly, the sound of Dex's voice erupted into the night. He had uncovered the recording device.

Fabi's heart began to race. Alexis was caught. Just then Dex's buddies approached, making all kinds of noise huffing, puffing, and bumping into tombs.

"Dude," one of the guys said, "that little guy got away."

"What do you mean?" Dex asked.

"He was just too quick — he rushed into traffic. Yo, what are we doing here, anyway?"

"This slut here was recording me," Dex said.

His voice was dark and heavy. "She tried to trick me. I think we need to teach her a lesson."

"Dex, wait. Let me explain. It's not my fault," Alexis pleaded.

"Well, let's hurry up, then," said one of the guys. "I don't like this place."

"Yeah, man, it's kind of spooky," another voice added.

"What are you ladies afraid of?" Dex teased. "Scared of the boogeyman?" He started to laugh.

"Nah, it's not that, but you know. There are ghosts here. My mom has seen them. For real!"

"You guys are idiots. Now, find something to tie her with."

"No," Alexis cried out.

Fabiola's heart was beating wildly, but she didn't know what to do. All she had was a stupid headlamp. She looked on the ground around her and saw a big piece of cement. It was part of a tomb that had crumbled off. Maybe she could knock one of the guys out with it. She motioned for Milo to grab a rock.

[165]

Fabi could hear Alexis struggle. The sounds tore at her core. She couldn't restrain herself and jumped out from behind the tomb, screaming at the top of her lungs. The two guys holding Alexis screamed, too, and leapt back in fright. They tried to run from Fabi, but a second figure in glowing gray appeared from the darkness and lurched at them with a long white sickle.

"*La Santa Muerte!*" Dex's friends shouted.

Dex stood frozen, eyes wide in disbelief. He watched, stunned, as the ghostly figure dissipated before his eyes. Then he shook himself, noticed his friends running away, and started to sprint as fast as his feet could take him, not looking back.

Fabiola rushed over to Alexis, shining her headlamp brightly over her. Alexis was in a daze, but fine.

Georgia Rae hurried up to them and cried, "Oh, Fabi, I am so sorry."

"What? You were great. Those guys were so afraid of you. I couldn't —"

Georgia Rae stared in confusion as she interrupted, "What? I didn't do anything. I got lost and couldn't find you until I heard Dex screaming."

"Huh? If you didn't jump out, and Milo was with me, then who?"

Alexis's eyes grew large. *"La Santa Muerte,"* she whispered, low enough for only them to hear.

A branch cracked to their left. They screamed at the top of their lungs as they raced out of the old cemetery.

chapter 11

Nothing was the same after that day.

At Garza's, Grandma Trini hijacked the jukebox and only played forlorn country ballads, bursting into tears at the end of each song. Leonardo went through the motions, creating his traditional classic dishes, but the food was on the bland side — lacking heart. Fabi's mother spent most of the day looking out the window, and she didn't even seem to notice the customers until they came up to pay. Additional duties were piling onto Fabiola's plate, but she didn't have the energy or desire to step up. The locals continued to come, but it was more out of habit.

All Fabiola could think about was how she failed. Dex and his buddies were free to bully and rob to their hearts' content. There was nothing she could do to change that. Tomorrow, Santiago would be taken to court and it was a hundred percent likely that he would go to jail for a really, *really* long time. The idea of Santiago locked up felt completely foreign to her. Every time the door chimed, she turned, expecting to see her cousin's crooked smile at the entrance of the restaurant.

Fabi sighed and looked across the dining room. Alexis was bouncing their baby brother on her knee. She looked up and smiled back. The "*Santa Muerte* sighting," as it would henceforth be referred to in local folklore, united the sisters like never before. They were different people in many ways, but they would always be sisters.

Tomorrow they were going to close the

restaurant so that everyone could go to Santiago's hearing. Fabiola couldn't remember the last time her father closed the restaurant. But like Leonardo always said, "Family is family. The Garzas stick together, for better or worse."

Fabi looked at the stack of schoolbooks under the counter, still waiting for her to read. How was she going to get through it all? Just then Fabi received a text message. She didn't recognize the number. It said:

If you want to save your cousin follow this link.

Fabi's heart jumped. "I need a computer!" she cried.

The little courtroom downtown was standing room only. Sunlight streamed in, illuminating the thin gray hair of Judge Dexter Andrews II. Dex's grandfather was a sickly old man, a shell of his former glory shrouded in black, sitting at the front of the room behind a heavy oak desk. Contrary to his feeble appearance, the man pounded hard on his gavel, ordering everyone to settle down.

"If I don't get some respect in my court-room, I will cancel the hearing and have you all escorted out of here," he yelled, turning blotchy red as if he had a bad case of hives. The threat seemed to work, and the audience quieted down.

Still, when Santiago entered the room, family and friends jumped from their seats in a big commotion. People shouted his innocence. Girls promised to wait for him. His mother threatened to put him over her knee for a good old-fashioned spanking. The grandmothers leaned over the railing holding sealed Tupperware containers of his favorite foods. The bailiff came around to collect the containers to hold them for Santiago.

Magda leaned over and whispered in Alexis's ear, "Where's your sister? She should have been here an hour ago."

Alexis checked her cell again, in case there

was another message. "She said she was on her way."

"But that was an hour ago."

"I know, but she needed to borrow a laptop." Alexis kept glancing at the back door. The waiting was killing her. Her heart sank when the judge began to read the charges. She couldn't believe this was happening. Where was Fabiola?

"Santiago Reyes, how do you plead to the charges of assault and battery, robbery, breaking and entering, and possession of stolen goods?" the judge asked in his gravelly voice. It sent shivers up Alexis's spine.

Alexis glanced over her shoulder and saw Dex, who had escorted the judge, his grandfather, into the courtroom. Now Dex was standing in the back corner of the courtroom with his arms crossed. He was wearing a sinister smirk. She had tried to avoid him all week, but Dex and his friends wanted to make an example of her. They circulated false rumors of sexual exploits around school like the evening news, and taunted her in the halls excessively. Now Dex caught her looking at him and mockingly blew her a kiss.

"I'd like to plead half and half," Santiago said in a joking manner. The crowd exploded in laughter and the judge pounded loudly, threatening again to throw everyone out if they didn't hush. When the crowd settled, Santiago explained, "Okay, so maybe those hubcaps were stolen, but I didn't steal them. I found them. So if you want to bust me for finding things, then you're going to have to bust a lot of other people in this town, too. As far as breaking and entering, I had the key and maybe I broke some plates, but I didn't think that was a serious offense. But I swear to you, Mr. Judge, sir, that I did not touch Chuy or any of those other guys, either. I didn't."

The judge angrily waved his mallet in Santiago's direction. "You think this is all a joke, don't you? You like making a mockery of this court? Think it'll be funny if I try you as an adult? Think going to prison is a joke, son?"

Santiago's eyes widened. He started to sweat. "No, sir," he said in a timid voice.

"What?! What did you say?" The judge cupped his hand over his ear.

"*No,* sir!" Santiago repeated, louder.

Friends and family went up to the witness stand to give testimony of Santiago's character. His teachers, family, and soccer coach spoke. Most of the stories were pretty funny, but inadvertently, they all ended up with Santiago getting in trouble.

"Ten years from now," the judge said, gathering his papers in front of him as if getting ready to go, "you're going to thank me, boy. Ten years from now you may have grown some manners."

"*Ten years!*" Alexis choked back, coughing uncontrollably.

"Excuse me, Your Honor!" a familiar voice interrupted from the back of the room. It was Fabi. She was holding a laptop computer in her right hand. "If you please, I have evidence here that will prove beyond a shadow of a doubt that Santiago did not mug Chuy."

"Who are you?" the judge asked, annoyed.

Fabi snaked her way through the crowd. "I'm Fabiola Garza, Santiago's cousin."

"This hearing has gone on long enough," he complained. "I will have no more shenanigans in my courtroom."

"Sir, you're really going to want to see this," she said, still holding up the computer.

The judge invited Fabiola to his office to view the evidence. She set the laptop on the desk. Fabi noted a picture of Dex, from elementary school, smiling brightly, next to the judge's stapler. She hesitated. This was Dex's grandfather. Dex had parents and family parties just like Santiago. Fabi felt bad for the judge.

The old man frowned. "I hope you're not wasting my time, young lady."

She pressed PLAY and the computer screen lit up in action. The video was not the best quality. It was taken from across the street and from a cell phone. But with the light from the streetlamp in front of Garza's restaurant you could clearly make out three guys with short hair beating up on a smaller man wearing a dirty apron.

"There's Chuy, the guy who was attacked, on the ground."

The judge said nothing, studying the three large men kicking Chuy from above. They all had short hair. Standing five feet away was another guy. It was obvious that he knew the attackers, because he didn't stop it. But he didn't participate, either.

One of the attackers stopped, looked over his shoulder, and said, "What's your problem?"

The guy hesitated before calling out, "I'm cool."

"No," the main attacker said, "get your ass over here and hit him. You're either with us or —"

"I don't want to."

"What is wrong with you?"

The guy shook his head, his hood fell off, and he ran. The video footage followed him down the block, clearly capturing the word "Dex" shaved into the back of his head. The cameraperson chased after him. But the angle was all wrong and captured the muzzle of some ratty dog with a sparkly collar. The video ended and Fabi took a deep breath. The judge thanked her for the evidence and asked her to leave.

epilogue

Fabiola stood in front of a two-story, Spanish-style, million-dollar home. She'd heard rumors that celebrity country singers and Mexican movie stars lived in this neighborhood, and secretly hoped to see someone famous. The splattering sound of water from the huge concrete fountain overpowered the chattering mockingbirds hidden inside the canopy of palm trees that encircled the estate.

Fabi took a deep breath to calm her nerves, combed her fingers through her loose hair, and pushed the doorbell. A dog started to bark inside. Through the stained-glass double doors she could see a shadowy figure jumping around. "Coming!" a voice called out over the noise.

Melodee Stanton opened the door. She flinched, and then made a disgusted expression as she said, "Oh, it's you." She was holding her mini Chihuahua in her arms. The dog, wearing a sparkly collar, snarled loudly at Fabi.

"Hi, Melodee," Fabi said, feeling her heart race. "I just came over to thank you."

"For what?"

Fabi could feel her face getting hot. Had she made a mistake? "For the video you sent me."

Melodee rolled her eyes. "I don't know what you've been smokin', but I didn't send anything. I don't even know your stupid phone number."

"I must have made a mistake."

"Yes, you obviously did."

"I'm sorry to bother you."

"Whatever." She rolled her eyes again and started to close the door.

But Fabiola grabbed on to the handle to stop her. "Oh, and I'm sorry about Dex. I know he meant a lot to you."

"That fool." Melodee made a "whatever" gesture with her hand. "Military school will be good for him. Teach him some manners. Now, I would love to stand here and chat all day, but I have better things to do."

"Yeah, sure. Well, thanks, anyway." Fabiola waved as she walked away. She didn't quite understand what had happened, but she was glad she'd at least tried to do the right thing by coming over here.

Fabiola Garza walked slowly toward her cousin's truck down the street. She could feel Melodee Stanton's eyes on her back. Looking forward, she noticed dark thundering clouds threatening to bring heavy showers.

She didn't know what the future held for her in this crazy small town, but she was ready to take it on.

acknowledgments

Border Town owes its existence to all the people who believe in multicultural teen literature. First, I would like to acknowledge and thank my fabulous agent and friend, Stephanie Von Borstel. I also thank my amazing editor, Amanda Maciel, and the entire Scholastic team for their enthusiastic support, trust, and commitment to this series. I wish to thank my super-cool *familia*, Mom, Dad, Bill, Suni, and the rest of the Ramírez clan — you rock! And I thank my fantastic crew of readers, Tracy *"La*

Inspectora" Baxter, Hermilo *"El Guapo"* Guzman III, and Matthew *"El Ojo"* Armburst.

This book would not be possible without the love and support of friends, teachers, librarians, and students of the Rio Grande Valley. I specifically wish to acknowledge Elizabeth Muñoz, Liza Lara, Juan and Maria Elena Ovalle, *la familia Avila*, Cynthia Perales, Moses Castillo, and Sarah Cuadra. Thank you for sharing your homes, your stories, and your *Valle conmigo*.

Tex-Mex for Beginners

abuelita: grandma

Ándale: Go. / Hurry up. / Move.

Aquí es: Here it is. / It's here.

basta: enough

carne asada: grilled steak

cárteles: short for "drug cartel"; a criminal organization that promotes and transports illegal drugs

chanclas: flip-flops, sandals, slippers

chifladas: crazy, wild, hootchie

chile con carne: meat with red chili pepper sauce

comadre: a good woman friend

comal: cooking plate, skillet

Con esa gente no se juega: You don't play around with those people.

conjunto: literally "group"; a musical group, usually a Norteño or Tex-Mex musical group

copete: pompadour; hair styled to stand up above forehead

diablo: devil

Dos Rios: Two Rivers

el valle: the valley

En el nombre del Padre: literally "In the name of the Father"; the Lord's Prayer

Estás loca: You're out of your mind.

fresas: literally "strawberries"; also someone who is a snob, stuck-up, upper class

gorda: chubby

guapa: pretty, elegant woman

huercos: literally "pigs"; used to refer to kids

la lechuza: literally "owl"; witches who transform into owls/birds; if you see one it's a bad omen and means someone's going to die

la mafia: Mexican Mafia

la pulga: flea market

la Santa Muerte: Saint Death

limpia: cleaning, cleansing (physical or spiritual)

los Dedos del Valle: literally "the Fingers of the Valley"; name implies a good accordionist

maleducada: literally "badly raised"; rude

mentirosa: liar

menudo: tripe stew

mija: short for "*mi hija*"—my daughter

mojaditos: literally means "little wet ones"; used to refer to undocumented immigrants

nada: nothing, a nobody

norteño: northern Mexican cowboy style

pan dulce: sweet bread

picante: spicy, hot, racy

piruja: loose woman, floozie, prostitute

Por el árbol se conoce el fruto: The apple doesn't fall far from the tree.

quinceañera: literally "15-year-old"; commonly refers to Sweet 15 birthday party

raspas: short for *"raspados"*; shaved ice with flavored syrup

sinvergüenza: shameless

tapada: stopped up, constipated

tapón: plug, stopper

tía: aunt

un viejo amor: an old love, lover, flame

[The Border Town drama continues in *Quince Clash*.]

Melodee began to laugh, but then stopped. She stared Fabi in the eye, as if trying to drill a hole to the truth. "All right," she said with a nod. "You think your quince will be better than mine? It's on. You and me." She pointed to Fabi. "We'll have a quinceañera competition. And everyone here will vote."

Fabi felt the blood drain from her face. She never wanted a quinceañera in the first place. Now she had to have one—and not just any quinceañera. Fabi had to have the biggest, best quince the Valley had ever seen.